The Day the World

Stopped Turning

THE DAY THE WORLD STOPPED TURNING

Michael Morpurgo

Feiwel and Friends
New York

A Feiwel and Friends Book
An imprint of Macmillan Publishing, LLC
120 Broadway, New York, NY 10271

THE DAY THE WORLD STOPPED TURNING.

Our books may be purchased in bulk for promotional, educational, or business use.
Please contact your local bookseller or the Macmillan Corporate and Premium Sales Department
at (800) 221-7945 ext. 5442 or by email at MacmillanSpecialMarkets@macmillan.com.

Library of Congress Control Number: 2018955769
ISBN 978-1-250-10707-7 (hardcover) / ISBN 978-1-250-10708-4 (ebook)

First published in 2018 in Great Britain as *Flamingo Boy* by HarperCollins Children's Books,
a division of HarperCollinsPublishers Ltd.

First published in the United States of America by Feiwel and Friends,
an imprint of Macmillan Publishing Group, LLC

Book design by Rebecca Syracuse
Feiwel and Friends logo designed by Filomena Tuosto

First U.S. edition, 2019
1 3 5 7 9 10 8 6 4 2

mackids.com

For Alan, for Lorens,
and their mum and dad

*With thanks to Anne-Sophie Deville, who first
introduced us to her flamingos and to the beauty
and mystery of her beloved Camargue*

CHAPTER 1

Someone Called Vincent

I read it in a book once, when I was a boy. I don't remember what book it was from, but the story I have never forgotten. An old traveler is sitting on the steps of his gypsy caravan, drinking a mug of tea in the sunshine. He's stopped for awhile, right in the middle of a roundabout, his tethered piebald horse grazing the grass verge nearby.

A police car pulls up. "You can't stop here," the policeman says.

"Morning, son," says the traveler. "You want some tea? Got plenty to spare." The policeman is rather nonplussed by this. No one has called him "son" for a very long time, and he rather likes it.

"No time to stop for tea," he says. "Thanks all the same. Where are you going, you and your horse?"

"Not sure," says the traveler. "The old horse and me, we just follow the bend in the road, go wherever it takes us."

"Nice horse," the policeman says, his tone softening all the time.

"And where might you be off to, son, this fine day?" the old traveler asks him.

"Maybe I'll do what you do," replies the policeman. "Maybe I'll just follow the bend in the road. Sounds like a good idea." And off he goes, knowing full well he should have moved the old traveler on, but glad he hadn't.

I don't know why, but I have never forgotten that story. I am older these days, a lot older—over fifty now. And, when I think about it, I suppose that in my own way I was trying to do just what the old traveler had done, what that policeman said he would like to do. I was following the bend in the road. That's what I was setting out to do, in the summer of 1982, which was a long time ago now, but I remember it all, as if it were yesterday. It's another story I don't forget. You don't forget the stories and the people who change your life.

It began with a picture, a painting, two paintings really. In Art class at my primary school, Miss Weatherby—who was the best teacher I ever had—told us one day to "paint a story." So I painted a picture of that same old traveler sitting on the steps of his gypsy caravan, his piebald horse grazing the grass nearby, and there was a police car in the painting too. I gave it a title, wrote it at the top: *Following the Bend in the Road.* Miss Weatherby said it was the best painting I had ever done— she said that a lot, but she meant it every time. I took it home. My mother also said it was brilliant, so brilliant that I should sign it, and she would hang it up on the wall in my bedroom, in pride of place, next to my boat picture.

Now, that other picture, the boat picture, is very important in the story, because my name is Vincent, Vincent Montague. Only my mother called me Vincent. My friends at school always called me "Monty," or "Vince," neither of which I have ever liked. I always liked to be known as Vincent. So, of course, I signed my picture "Vincent."

My mother had it framed—she liked it that much—and hung it, as she said she would, on the wall above my bed. "There is only one place for this," I remember her saying, as she stood back, head to one side, and admired it. "It looks perfect up there, doesn't it? That's just where it belongs."

So there it was, my picture of the old traveler, hanging right beside my boat picture, the one that had always been there above my bed, that I had always loved: a painting of four boats on a beach, with the sea and sky behind. Strangely, it was also signed by "Vincent," which was, of course, I am sure, one of the reasons why I had always loved it so much. But I hadn't painted that one. Someone else had, someone else called Vincent.

My mother used to joke about it sometimes. "I like that boat picture, Vincent," she would laugh, "but I prefer yours." I loved her saying that, of course, but for years I never understood why it was that funny. I just thought she had a rather strange sense of humor, which was true. Anyway, both of these pictures became part of the land-scape of my life as I grew up, from a carefree primary-school kid who loved cycling and camping, into a sixth-form stu-dent who loved poetry and dreaming—and still camping—and was looking forward impatiently to whatever was coming next.

Gazing out of the window, which I so often did whilst I was supposed to be studying for my exams, down into the tiny walled garden of our suburban house in Watford, I might be absorbed for minutes on end watching a thrush cracking open a snail on the top of the wall. Everything and anything was more interesting to me than getting on with my work, even the washing line that was strung from the drainpipe on the garage across the garden to the weathervane on the shed, with pajamas and shirts flapping in the wind; or perhaps my mother would be home after work, chatting over the wall to Mrs. Donaldson next door, both of them out for a crafty smoke.

I was locked into interminable revision for my exams, dreading the day they would come, but longing to have them done and dusted, longing to have a life. I loved home, loved my mother, but I knew it was a small world I was living in, and I yearned to be gone, to be away from Watford, and off on my travels, to be following the bend in the road, like the old traveler in the story.

CHAPTER 2

My Near-Death Experience

In these idling moments, which were many, I kept finding myself turning again and again to look at the two pictures above my bed. I was trying so hard not to become distracted, but I never tried hard enough. Sooner or later, I always found I could no longer resist the temptation. I had to look.

There they were, my small gypsy caravan painting, my best painting ever, according to Miss Weatherby—the story behind it still echoing in my mind—and beside it the other "Vincent" picture. This was a much larger one in a heavy wooden frame, of four boats drawn up on the beach, and four more out at sea beyond—fishing boats by the look of them, but like no other boats I had ever seen. And both pictures painted by "Vincent." I am sure that my mother must have told me who this other Vincent was at some time or another in all these years; but, if she had, I hadn't been listening, or I wasn't interested, or I had long since forgotten.

It wasn't just the coincidence of the name that I loved. I loved the boat picture above any other paintings I had ever seen. They were graceful-looking boats, flamboyantly colored, in reds and blues and yellows and greens like the gypsy caravan in my own painting. The empty beach behind them stretched away to the horizon, waves rolling up onto the sand, and a wide, wide sky above was filled with scudding clouds. One of the boats was called *Amitié*—I could see it quite clearly painted on the prow.

The truth is that if I had not been so busy procrastinating that day, during my revision, I might have never discovered what that word meant at all. It was all part of my dreamy disinclination to get on and revise. I decided to look it up. It was a French word apparently, which I thought it might be—though I had never come across it in my French lessons. It meant "friendship" or "love." So I surmised these boats must very likely have been drawn up on a French beach, but where, on what coast, I had no idea.

At about the same time as I was making this discovery, I happened to come across—in a secondhand bookstall in town—another painting signed by this Vincent, of sunflowers. It was on the cover of a book, and it was a picture I knew at once. The signature was definitely the same, the bright and vibrant colors of the painting instantly recognizable too. I was sure it had to be painted by the same Vincent who had signed my boat picture. I still don't know what took me so long to get around to making the connection. I have to say I felt rather ignorant and stupid, because this Vincent was, of course, rather famous; in fact, he was amongst the most famous artists the world has ever known. I bought the book for £1.50, took it home, and read it from cover to cover.

Vincent van Gogh, a Dutch artist, had signed his pictures "Vincent," just as I had signed my gypsy caravan painting. I might have recognized his famous sunflower picture, but I had never before paid any attention to the signature, nor really taken on board who it was that had painted these amazing sunflowers. And I certainly did not know he had painted fishing boats as well. But there it was on the wall above my bed, my boat picture, and painted by the famous Vincent van Gogh.

He had spent some time in the South of France, I discovered, toward the end of his life. Whilst living there, he had painted hundreds of pictures, some landscapes, some of the people who lived and worked there. A few of them—including mine—he had painted down by the sea, just a few miles from where he was living, in a town called Arles. It was in his room in Arles, in a state of deep depression, that he had cut off his own ear. Mental illness had forced him to spend time in a nearby hospital, but he never really recovered. In the end, he had been driven to suicide.

The more I read about him, the more I wanted to find out about him, to see as many of his pictures as I could, to go where he had gone, to stand on the beach where he had painted his boats. Such diversion and reveries, of course, did not help me to focus on revision for my Geography and English Literature exams, and even less on my Biology, which I especially loathed.

But it wasn't just my belated discovery of who this

Vincent was that made me want to go where he had gone, to find the beach where he had painted my picture of the fishing boats on the sand. There were other pictures from the book I particularly liked: one of a little bridge over a canal, and the one of a café bathed in yellow light in a cobbled street under a starry evening sky. I wanted to go to all these places, be where he had been. It wasn't because he was famous that made me want to go, and it wasn't just because we happened to share the same name either. It was because that boat picture of his above my bed very nearly killed me.

I was in my bedroom, at my desk by the window, pretending to be deep into my revision. Moments before, I had been lying on my bed, trying to summon up the willpower to get on with my work. I was only at my desk at all because I had heard my mother coming up the stairs and did not want her to catch me lazing about again. So there I was, hunched over my Biology textbook, looking as studious as I could, and waiting for the inevitable knock on my door. That was when it happened, my near-death experience. No crashing, no splintering of glass. The boat painting—I remind you, it was a large and very heavy picture—simply fell off the wall and landed with a great thud on my pillow, exactly where my head had been less than a minute before.

One look behind the picture told me that the string had broken, and that same look told me something else I had never known. There was a piece of paper taped to the back of the frame, covered in faded writing. I picked the picture up and carried it over to the light of the window so I could read it.

To little Vincent from his grandma and grandpa, on your first birthday, 27th January 1964.

A long time ago, we went to this beach in the Camargue region in the South of France, where Vincent van Gogh had gone when he painted this picture. The boats were not there, of course, but the beach and the sea and the sky were just as he painted them. It was windy that day, and you can almost feel the wind in his picture. We bought it at a local shop and had it hanging in our bedroom for years and years. It is our favorite picture in all the world. So we thought you might love it too, as much as we have. And, you never know, one day you might go to the Camargue, and stand on the beach where we once stood, in the wind, where another Vincent, Vincent van Gogh, painted these lovely boats.

With our love always,

G and G

Had that picture not fallen off the wall, none of the rest of this story would have happened at all, a story that in the end would turn out to have very little to do with Vincent van Gogh. But without him and his boat painting that nearly killed me that day, and without Grandma and Grandpa I suppose, I would never have chosen to go on my travels, after my exams were over, down to the South of France where Vincent van Gogh had once gone.

I went on my wanderings by train and bus, and on foot, camping out, always following the bend in the road, a road that I hoped might lead me eventually down toward the sea, and maybe even to the beach where Vincent van Gogh had painted those fishing boats all those years before. It was a road that would take me instead into another world, into another time and another place altogether.

CHAPTER 3

The Long, Straight Road to Nowhere

So it was that I found myself that first summer of freedom wandering my way through the strange and mysterious landscape of the Camargue in the South of France, marveling at the windswept wildness of the marshes around me, at the shallow pink lakes and the canals, at the ancient stone farmhouses, and, everywhere, flocks of flamingos. Every sighting of them lifted my spirits for, beautiful though this place was, it was desolate too and inhospitable, especially when the wind howled and roared, which it did sometimes for days on end. All I could do then was huddle in my tent, and hope against hope that it would not blow me away.

When at last the wind did die down, the mosquitoes

would be there in their millions—every one of them, it seemed to me, homing in on my tent, seeking me out. Sleep was impossible. Cursing them, flailing at them, did not help—it made things worse, if anything. I covered my face and neck and arms and hands with the insect repellent my mother had made me take in my rucksack, along with pills for just about every illness I might encounter on my travels. But, as it turned out, none of the medicines she had given me was of much help when I most needed it.

I don't know whether it was the water I had drunk that made me ill, or something I had eaten, or some kind of infection from the mosquito bites I had been scratching. I do know that one evening, walking down a long, straight road to nowhere, as it seemed to me, a causeway with pink lakes on both sides, and not a bend in sight, I began to feel strange, as if I were no longer part of myself. My head was full of a throbbing pain that weighed heavy on my forehead. I kept having bouts of dizziness that brought me near to losing my balance, to fainting. Sometimes it felt as if my legs were not my own, that they were stumbling on by themselves, and not under my control at all.

I remember there were flamingos nearby, strolling languidly through the shallows, lifting their heads between feeding and peering at me quizzically as I passed by. The mosquitoes were gone and I was thankful for that, but then I felt the dreaded wind coming in again, in vicious gusts, trying to blow me off the causeway into the lake. I shouted at the wind to go away, and the flamingos took off in a flurry of beating wings and honking, leaving me alone on the road.

"Not you!" I cried to them. "I didn't mean you. Come back! Please come back!" But they did not. Now I had only the cruel wind for company.

I knew I needed help, but there was no one about, not a house in sight, and the road behind and ahead of me went on forever, as far as I could see, into the gathering gloom of the evening, daylight lingering now only in distant streaks of sunset. The lakes on either side of me were no longer pink but bloodred. But then, to my great relief, the flamingos returned. They came flying over my head, floating in on wide black wings to land nearby, in their hundreds, honking happily at me, telling me, I thought, to keep going. So I did, somehow. They seemed to be walking along with me, through the shallows, escorting me, on either side of the road.

I marveled at the elegance of these creatures, at the oddness of their balletic gait, and their absurd, outsize curved bills, at the incongruity of their startling pinkness. Their sticklike legs seemed to be wading backward through the water, and yet, impossibly, they were moving forward. There was no logic to their knee joints. Their bills were fishing backward too. How did they do that? They could stand one-legged in this wild wind and not fall over. They ran on water to take off and land. How did they do that?

My legs were giving way under me, becoming weaker now with every step. I knew they must collapse at any moment. My senses were reeling, my head swirling, my knees buckling. The flamingos nearby were looking at me in astonishment, honking to me, calling to me. I felt myself blacking out, falling, and there was nothing I could do about it.

There is a time between sleeping and waking when dreams are at their most intense and real, so much so that you cannot be sure that the dreamtime has ended or the waking has begun. Dream or not, there was an evening sky above me, and I was lying awkwardly, uncomfortably, on my back, on stony ground. A dog was snuffling at my ear. I was sure it was a dog, because it smelled like dog, and its nose was cold and wet on my ear. The honking of the flamingos echoed through my dream, calling me awake.

Gentle fingers were opening my eyelids, stroking my hair and touching my cheek. An urgent voice was calling to me, but not with any words I could understand. I was still desperately trying to remain cocooned in my dream, unable or unwilling to wake. I was being lifted then. I could hear grunting, heavy breathing, stumbling footsteps. I knew I was being carried, but whether this was all happening in my dream or not I still had no idea, and neither did I care.

I heard the howling of the wind, felt the cold of it on my cheek. Only then did I really begin to believe that I might be coming out of my dream. I felt strong arms around me. I *was* being carried. Whoever it was who had rescued me was struggling to keep going, groaning and staggering with the effort of it. But still I could make no proper sense of what was going on around me. My rescuer seemed sometimes to be speaking to me with the gentle honking voice of a flamingo, but then out of the honking came strange and unintelligible words: "Renzo Renzo." He kept repeating these same words over and over again. I gave up trying to understand what he was saying, what was happening to me, and soon slipped back into the comforting world of oblivion.

CHAPTER 4

Renzo Renzo

I was warm through when I finally woke. I found myself lying on some kind of a couch, by a crackling fire, with logs blazing, a dog lying at my feet, his nose close to the burning embers. Sitting opposite me at a small table was a woman, a flowery shawl around her shoulders, her hair gathered into a silvery bun. I could not see her face, because her head was bent. She was intent on writing in a notebook, and did not look up. I never saw hair so silver.

The dog stirred and scratched vigorously, which was when she did look up, and noticed I was awake. She spoke in French, which puzzled me at first. I was still muddle-headed, I suppose, not knowing quite where I was nor how

I had got here. For some moments, in my confused state, I just stared at her, until my memories gathered themselves, and fell more into place. I could remember now the walk along the long road to nowhere, the flamingos on either side of me, the pink lakes, my throbbing head, the man carrying me who seemed to be honking like a flamingo.

The woman was speaking English to me now as she put down her writing book and leaned forward. She had a heavy accent, but her English was quite understandable.

"You prefer that I speak English? I hope you will forgive me, but I looked in your bag to find out who you were," she said. "And I found this, your passport." She picked it up from the table beside her, to show me, and opened it. "You are Vincent Montague. Yes? A British passport, so you are a British flamingo, *non*?" She could see I was bewildered at this, and smiled. "Lorenzo, he will be so pleased he found you. Usually, he brings back a French flamingo, or an egret maybe, or a frog or a rabbit, or a terrapin, but they are always French. You are the first British flamingo he has ever brought home!"

I must still have been looking puzzled. She went on to

explain. "Lorenzo—Renzo he calls himself—is the one who found you half dead on the road. He likes always to keep an eye out for his flamingos. He loves his flamingos. In spring, he likes to be sure no one is out there stealing their eggs. Very few do these days, but he likes to keep watch, just in case. And now, in summer, there are always fledglings, who sometimes become separated from their mothers, and are too weak to survive. So he is on the lookout for them too. He is out there on the marshes, patrolling most nights. He told me it was the dog who found you— Ami, we call him— which means 'friend' in English, but I expect you know this. You speak a little French, perhaps?" I shook my head. I knew some French from school, but had never dared to speak it, and I did not want to have to start now.

"It does not matter," she went on. "You are English—I did not expect anything else. Lorenzo tells me he carried you home. A long way, he said, and you were heavy too, but he is strong. Years of work on the farm, it makes you strong. I have made you soup, and I have some cheese also. And you must drink water, lots of water. Water is the great healer."

She got up then, and put her notebook down on the table beside her. "I will tell Renzo you are awake." She came and laid the back of her hand against my forehead. "You are better, but still too hot. Water," she went on, picking up a glass on the table beside me. "It is empty. You will need more water. Renzo will bring some for you. He is the doctor. You are his patient. I am just the nurse." She walked away then, calling for him. "Renzo! Renzo!"

I was left alone with Ami, who was a very large brown dog. He sat by my knee now, gazing up at me.

"So it was you who found me," I said, reaching out rather nervously and patting the top of his head. He was shaggy all over, his dark eyes glinting at me from deep inside his matted fur. "Thank you for finding me," I said to him. "*Merci.*"

"*Merci merci,*" came an echoing voice from the door. The man who stood there filled the doorway. He was holding a glass of water, but he did not seem to want to come into the room, and kept repeating "*merci*" over and over again. The dog got up and walked to him, tail high and waving. But he paid it no attention. The man's eyes were fixed on me, unwavering, unblinking. There was nothing alarming about his gaze. It was steady, not staring. He was scrutinizing me, I felt, much in the same way as I was examining him.

Everything about him was long and tall. His arms hung loose at his sides. He had sloping shoulders under his blue jacket, and huge hands, I noticed. There was light in the room only from the flickering fire and from the oil lamp on the table where the woman had been writing, so I could not see his face that well. He did not seem to want to talk, but simply stood there, considering me. I said nothing, because I could not think of anything to say. I turned to gaze into the fire.

The woman with the silver hair came in awhile later, carrying a tray. "This is Lorenzo," she said. "He does not say much. He speaks more with his eyes, don't you, Renzo?"

"Renzo," he said, coming slowly toward me. "Renzo Renzo." He was tapping the side of his head as he spoke; and then, breaking into a sudden loud laugh of delight, he bent down and picked up my hand, but not to shake as I supposed. He lifted it to his nose. He was smelling my hand. His face was close to mine then, his nose almost touching my hair. He was smelling that too, then stroking it, and smelling his own hand afterward.

"You must not worry. It is how he gets to know people," the woman explained. "You will find he is friendly to everyone who is kind. And he is never friendly to those who are not. He thinks you are kind, so you must be. Lorenzo is never wrong about people.

"*Oh, pardonnez-moi*—I am so sorry. I am being most impolite," she went on. "I am Kezia, Kezia Charbonneau. Lorenzo and I, we are like brother and sister, you could almost say. But we are best friends. *Meilleurs amis.* We grew up together, and now we look after each other, and the farm, and the flamingos, don't we? *N'est-ce pas, Renzo?*"

But this Lorenzo was not listening. He was still occupied totally with examining me, bending over me, his eyes peering deep into mine. I never saw eyes kinder nor more intense than his. He seemed to be seeking out my soul. It was troubling to me at first—no one had ever looked at me like this before. I was unsettled also by the hugeness of his presence so close to me, but there was an overwhelming sense of tenderness about him that banished all fear. He was no threat to me, but he was strange. He seemed like a middle-aged man, but had the open face of a boy.

Kezia set the tray down on the table beside me. The soup smelled wonderful, and there was bread and cheese beside it.

"Eat, Vincent, eat," she told me. "*Mangez.*"

"*Mangez mangez,*" Lorenzo echoed, and lifted his arms slowly, making great wings of them, and then he was honking just like a flamingo.

"This he always does when he is happy," Kezia said, smiling. I noticed her earrings then, like golden crescent moons they were, shining in the light of the fire. "Sometimes I think he is half Lorenzo, half flamingo," she went on. "He can walk like them too, talk like them. You will see."

"Flam flam!" Lorenzo was saying, clapping his hands excitedly. "Flam flam!" And then suddenly he was waving at me, saying good-bye. He turned away, opened the front door and left.

"Before he goes to bed, he has to see his beloved flamingos," Kezia went on, "the ones he has rescued, mostly young ones, chicks, fledglings. He looks after them in his shed, feeds them. There are other animals in there too. It is like a hospital. He likes to spend a little time there in the evenings with them, to say good night. Now, you must eat your soup, Vincent, before it gets cold."

She sat down again in her chair, watching me and smiling approvingly when she saw how much I was enjoying the soup. It was warming me from the roots of my hair down to my toes.

"You will stay with us until you are strong, Vincent," she said. "Lorenzo and me, we shall look after you, make you better. To him, you are like one of his lost fledgling flamingos, and to me you are a welcome guest. We shall not put you in his hospital shed, I promise you. He keeps it as clean as he can, but the creatures he looks after in there, they do smell, and you would not like it. You shall stay here in the house, by the fire. Between Lorenzo and me, we shall make you well again, you will see."

She smiled at me. "Vincent. It is a good name," she went on. "*Français aussi, vous savez.* It is a French name also."

"Where am I?" I asked her, looking about me.

"On a farm," she told me. "On a farm far out in the marshes, in the middle of nowhere, you could say, a few kilometers down the road, along the canal from a little town called Aigues-Mortes. Do you know this place? Have you been there?"

I shook my head. I was still bewildered, my head full of so many questions. "How come you speak English so well?" I asked her.

"*Ah ça, c'est une histoire.* That is a story, Vincent, a long story, one that I might tell you when I know you better. First, we have to make you well again. You must have lots of sleep, and peace and quiet. You will stay here with us for a few days and rest." She reached out and felt my forehead again. "You have a fever still. We shall have you better again, but it will take time. You cannot hurry a fever. No more questions. Sleep well. *Dormez bien.*"

CHAPTER 5

A Complete Flamingo

I don't think I had ever been properly ill before this in all my life. I had had a day or two off school with coughs and colds, but mostly with invented illnesses to avoid some lesson or test I didn't want to have to face. This was different. This was the real thing. My head ached, my legs ached, every part of me ached. I seemed one moment to be shivering uncontrollably with cold, and the next I was pouring with sweat—often both together. Night and day, I hovered on the cusp of sleep. In and out of my dreams, the wind seemed always to be blowing, whistling down the chimney, rattling the windows and shaking the shutters. And whenever I woke it always took some time for me to remember where I was now, what had happened, how I had got here. I still had little idea where I was.

But each day, whenever I woke, the faces I saw around me were becoming more familiar, more reassuring. One of them, either Kezia or Lorenzo, was always nearby, somewhere in the room, keeping an eye on me, waiting for me to wake. And, more often than not, Ami would be lying there by the fire, or would be sitting right by me, eyeing me through his fur. Kezia might be sitting in her chair opposite, mending clothes or writing in her notebook. When Lorenzo was there, he would be close to me, his hand resting often on my hair, his eyes closed. Sometimes I would wake up and find him blowing gently on my forehead, humming softly to me. When he noticed I was awake, or saw my eyes open, he would at once spring to his feet, clapping his hands with delight, calling to Kezia to come. Often, all three were there, waiting for me to wake, and I could feel them willing me well again.

All around me, on the walls, there were photographs. From where I lay, I thought I could recognize Kezia and Lorenzo in some of them, as children. There were other people in the photographs I did not know, other family, I supposed. But many of the photographs were of animals: herds of black bulls and white horses, some sheep too. Most though were of flamingos, large and small, and these were all in color: flamingos flying across the sky in great flocks, or landing on the water, or standing alone and majestic in the marshes, or sitting on nests, or feeding in the shallows. I longed to be able to get up and look more closely. But I was still too weak to do it on my own. Even going to the toilet, I still needed one of them to steady me, to help me walk across the room.

But I could already feel myself getting better. I did not shiver anymore, nor break into cold sweats. I slept less and my energy was beginning to return. I was feeling stronger with every day that passed. I wanted to test my legs, my balance, get myself moving. I was beginning to wander about the room, peer out of the windows, look at the photographs close up, all the while trying to make more sense of my surroundings. The room where I had been lying night and day on my couch was cavernous, with a high, heavily beamed ceiling. It was living room, kitchen, eating room all in one, and sparsely furnished—just my couch, a few chairs, a small table, a blanket for Ami by the fire. Everything was huddled close around the open fireplace, which was the glowing, crackling heart of the room.

There was a small kitchen in one corner, where Kezia was often busy over the stove, or the sink, and beyond the kitchen was the door to the bathroom, the only other room I'd been into. A staircase in the darkest corner of the room led upstairs to where Kezia and Lorenzo went each night, leaving Ami and me to the flickering warmth of the fire. There was no electricity in the house, so far as I could see. The house smelled of oil lamps and burning wood, and of whatever Kezia happened to be cooking on the stove. She made the best soups I had ever tasted, mostly vegetable soups, with potatoes or rice, and there was always bread, crusty, chewy, not at all like the bread at home. I loved it.

Outside, the wind often raged and roared about the house, and, when it did, it was continuous, unrelenting, for a week or more sometimes, and with such ferocity that the house shook. So loud was this wind, this mistral, as Kezia called it, that it was difficult to think straight at all, and sometimes impossible to hear what Kezia was saying in her still, small voice. Lorenzo I could hear better, despite the mistral, because he would often repeat the same word louder and louder for me. But understanding him was difficult. If ever I looked perplexed—and I was often perplexed—he would act out what he meant, which I could see he loved to do. But, even then, much of what he was trying to tell me was beyond my comprehension.

"Flam flam" was one of the things he said that needed no explanation. He spoke it more than any other, and it sometimes provoked in him an extraordinary metamorphosis. "Flam flam," he would say, and, on the spur of the moment, he would become a flamingo, a living, breathing flamingo, stepping out in long, slow, stiff strides across the room, leaning forward, his neck stretched out, bending to feed, scooping through the shallows, just as I had seen them out on the lakes in the marshes. Then his arms would suddenly open up and become wings, and he would be flying, soaring around the room. Whenever he did this, I would marvel at how such a large man, often so awkward in his mannerisms and movements, could glide about the room with such balletic grace, honking happily, a complete flamingo.

But there were so many other words he kept saying that I could not yet understand at all. He seemed to think that by repeating them louder, his face closer to mine, it might help me understand. I could sense his frustration and disappointment when I did not. So sometimes I would resort to pretending that I knew what he was talking about. But I don't think I ever fooled him. And anyway I sensed that he did not like me pretending. When she was there, Kezia would often see my difficulty and come to my rescue, interpreting for me. But she was not always around. So the meaning of many of his words remained a mystery to me.

"Rousel," "grette," "Capo," "Val," "Lot Lot"—these were just some of the words that he used, many of them quite often, words he clearly longed for me to understand. I could see he liked it when I repeated the words back to him. That was what made him happy. So that's what I did. He liked me to be an echo. And I also learned early on with Lorenzo that he liked truth, that for him pretending between people, unless it was for fun, was not truthful, and that upset him.

It took awhile for me to begin to understand this strange, awkward man, who seemed to live so much of every day in a world of his own. He was like no one I had ever encountered before. He joined our world—the real world as we like to think of it—and left it as and when he felt like it. Everything he did was both spontaneous and meant. His words and his ways were his own. I was getting used to his language, his moaning, or groaning, or humming, to his sudden shrieks and shouts of exuberance, his bursts of laughter and clapping. I noticed that Ami, if he could, would follow Lorenzo everywhere he went, walking at his heels. Unlike me, he seemed to understand every word Lorenzo spoke, every gesture and grunt. Kezia too, I could see, understood him instinctively. I envied the closeness among the three of them, the complete understanding and trust. I felt like an outsider sometimes, but they never treated me as such.

Lorenzo had his own way of ending the day. He would be gone for an hour or so out on the farm, saying good night to the animals in his hospital, I presumed, or patrolling the marshes, looking for waifs and strays. When he came in, he rarely sat down at all, even to eat, but liked to stay in the room with us while we did. He would stand, watching the fire in silence, usually nibbling on a piece of sausage— he ate almost nothing else but sausage. When the moment came that he decided to go to bed, it always took me by surprise, even though I was expecting it. He would turn away from us, stop to crouch down for awhile over Ami, touch him on his head, give him the last of his sausage, then, with a wave of his hand, walk very deliberately toward the stairs. As he went, he would lift his arms, make wide beating wings of them, and make his way upstairs, honking his farewell.

Kezia and I would sit and talk by the fire, or sit together for awhile in comfortable silence. I was by now much less tired than I had been.

There was so much I wanted to ask her, about Lorenzo especially, but also about the photographs on the walls too, who everyone in them was, how the two of them had come to be living here together. I had asked her once about how she had learned to speak English, but still she had not told me. I was longing to find out. I was intrigued about everything, and I knew that time was short. Now I was up and about a bit more—though I was not yet allowed out-side in that wind—I would soon have to think about leav-ing. I did not want to have to say good-bye before finding answers to all the whys and wherefores in my head.

I had asked her more than once as well about the pho-tographs on the walls, who everyone was, but Kezia simply said they were family, and would say nothing else. I felt that to ask again might be to intrude and upset her, and, after all she and Lorenzo had done for me, I did not want to do that.

CHAPTER 6

How It Was, How We Were

As it turned out, I never had to ask her at all. One evening, as we were sitting there by the fire, just after Lorenzo had gone up to bed, Kezia started asking me questions. "*Alors*, Vincent. You must tell me something about yourself," she said suddenly, quite unexpectedly. "In England, *en Angleterre*, where do you live? Have you any brothers or sisters at home? I know nothing about you. What have you been studying, Vincent? And what were you doing, by the way, wandering through the Camargue in the middle of the night? This I have always wanted to know."

I kept it short, told her only the essentials. I told her about home, about the boat picture on the wall in my bedroom, about how it had fallen off and nearly killed me, and the letter from my grandparents I had discovered on the back, about Vincent van Gogh and the Camargue, about my horrible exams, about how, once they were over, I had said good-bye to my mother, walked out of the door, rucksack on my back, free as a bird, and found my way down to the Camargue.

Her eyes, I noticed, lit up when I told her that. "Bravo! I see you have the Roma spirit in you," she said. "You are a wanderer, a traveler. I like that. And now that you have answered my questions, and I feel I know you a little better, maybe it is time for me to answer your question."

I did not know which question she meant. There were so many I wanted to ask by now. I must have looked rather blank.

"Vincent, you do not remember? You asked me how I learned to speak English so well. Maybe you do not wish to know?"

"No, no, please, I want to hear," I told her.

She sat back in her chair, hitched her shawl up around her shoulders, and looked across at me. "So much of everything that happens to us, Vincent, that makes our lives what they are, is just pure chance—*le hasard*, as we say in French. The families and times we are born into, the places we live. All chance. Think of it. Think of what happened to you. Because a picture falls off a wall, you find yourself wandering down a dark road to nowhere through the marshes of the Camargue, and you get sick, and Lorenzo happens to be out there with Ami on one of his evening patrols, looking for any abandoned fledgling flamingos, and they find you half dead on the road and bring you here. So here you are, and here I am, with Ami, and Lorenzo. *C'est le hasard*, Vincent, just chance.

"You know what they called Lorenzo when he was little, when I was little too, when I first knew him? Flamingo Boy. *En fait*, some people still do. You can understand why, I think. Lorenzo and me, we grew up here on this farm, together. We have known each other for almost all our lives. We were best friends from the day we met. And there was a very good reason for that. Lorenzo was different. I was different. It is not easy growing up different, not then, not now."

"I was wondering about that," I said. "I mean about Lorenzo's . . . well, about Lorenzo's difference."

"Listen, Vincent." She was reprimanding me now, with a frown and a wagging finger. "If you go on interrupting, I shall never even begin my story, let alone finish it, or I shall fall asleep telling it. You want to know everything, about Lorenzo, about us, about this farm. I understand that. You told me your story, which was quite short, but very interesting. So I shall tell you ours—that is only fair. But we are much older than you, both of us, and therefore it will take longer. I know from your passport you are just eighteen. Lorenzo and I, as I told you, we are the wrong side of fifty. So mine will be a longer story. *Alors*, Vincent, no more questions. Let me just tell you how it was, how we were, why I speak English, and why you find us together in this place.

"It is a little cold tonight. It is uncomfortable weather. Too hot in the day, and cold at night. Put a log or two on the fire, Vincent, and then just lie back, be quiet and listen. No more interruptions, agreed? *D'accord?*"

I did as I was told. Ami settled down to listen beside

me, his eyes, and mine, never leaving Kezia, as she looked into the fire and began.

"**R**enzo, Lorenzo Sully, was born upstairs, here in this farmhouse in the summer of 1932, on May the twenty-eighth. I remember this date rather well because I was born on the very same day, but not here. I was born thirty kilometers away, down by the sea. I am not sure exactly where, because being Roma people, traveling people—gypsies they call us in English, I think—my family was always on the move. So I was not to be part of Lorenzo's story until a few years later. We were not to meet until we were nine years old. Until then, I was traveling here, there, and everywhere, with Maman and Papa, in our caravan, setting up our carousel whenever and wherever they wanted us, on saints' days and holidays, at fairs and festivals in villages and towns all over the Camargue. That was our life.

Meanwhile, Lorenzo was growing up here on the farm with Nancy and Henri Sully, his *maman* and *papa*. They bred white horses and black bulls and kept some sheep too, for their wool and their meat and their cheese. They had speckled hens for their eggs. They gathered herbs from the countryside all around, and they fished in the lakes and streams and canals. And there were frogs there too. They had bees for honey. They grew some rice, potatoes, and beans, and also corn to feed the black bulls through the winter. It is only a small farm, about fifty hectares, and they did all the work themselves.

As you will hear, Nancy was later to become like an aunt to me—or more like a fairy godmother, I sometimes think. She told me often that, when Lorenzo was born, it was the greatest joy of their lives. He seemed a healthy child, always cheerful and loving. But then, when he was about two or three, they began to notice that he did not seem to want to get up and walk like other children, but sat there, watching the world go by. He was often bewildered and agitated, inconsolable sometimes, and for no reason they could understand. Neither was he learning to talk as other children did. Whenever they went into town, to Aigues-Mortes, which they did every week to set up their stall to sell their produce, other stallholders and customers would begin to comment on their beloved Lorenzo. They were not being deliberately unkind, but from time to time they did say that Lorenzo did not seem to be like other children.

Becoming more and more anxious about him as the years passed, and upset by some talk in the town that was not so kindly meant, Nancy took him at last to the town doctor, who examined him. He told her that Lorenzo was not developing as a normal child should, and informed her that there was an institution, in nearby Arles, for children like Lorenzo, where he could be cared for. When Nancy cried, the doctor simply said that these things happen, and that an institution was what would be best for the child. "Such strange and unnatural children," the doctor told her— and she never forgot his words—"do not belong amongst normal people in normal society."

These words, Nancy always said, stopped her tears. Anger stopped her tears. She told the doctor: "This is my child, our child, and he belongs with us." She never went to see that doctor again.

At home, on the farm, Lorenzo grew up strong and happy, in his own way, at his own speed. He learned to walk— though he was never as coordinated as other children. His legs and arms always seemed too long for him to manage, and he found it hard to run, but grow he did. He grew and he grew.

"He shot up as fast as a sunflower," Nancy told me once, "and just as beautiful too!"

Speech he also found difficult. But he loved to play with words, repeat them endlessly, rhythmically, whole sentences sometimes too, and he loved to sing, hum songs—words seemed to come easier to him when he sang them. Nancy and Henri soon realized he had a genius, a real genius, for imitating the sounds and movements of animals and birds, especially flamingos.

He loved above all else to be outside with Nancy and Henri on the farm. He was strong, so always happy to fetch and carry. He liked to feel useful. He would bring fodder and water to the animals, and loved to stay close to them, crouching down to watch them as they fed. Everyone noticed that horses, bulls, sheep, hens were always calm around him. The wildest of black bulls, the fiercest of the white stallions needed only to hear him humming, to feel his touch on their neck, his breath in their nostrils, and they were as gentle as lambs.

But it was the flamingos he loved to be with best of all. "Flam flam," Nancy always said, were the first words he ever spoke. He would sit down for hours on end, in his favorite place—on an upturned rowing boat by the side of a lake— looking out over the island, just to be with them. His great treat as a little boy was to be rowed by his *papa* out to the island to be near the little flamingo chicks, watching them finding their legs, trying their wings. He would call to them and they would come to him. He knew instinctively how to tread softly, move slowly, be still amongst them, and become one of them. He loved them, and they trusted him.

Whenever he came back in the boat, Nancy always told me, he would run about the farm like a flamingo, honking as they did, imitating their run through the shallows before takeoff, the spread of their great wide wings, the stretching of their necks in flight and then their elegant landing, his timing as perfect as theirs. Nancy told me once that when Lorenzo was being a flamingo he was at his happiest, that he became who he really was, his natural self.

And Lorenzo loved to ride. It was often the best way to get around the farm anyway, to move the bulls or see the brood mares, or to gather in the sheep, and, of course, to see the flamingos in the lakes all around. So whenever one of them went out on the horse—usually it was Henri—Lorenzo always had to go with him, whatever the weather, whatever the time of day. He loved to be up on that horse—Cheval, Lorenzo always called him—clinging on behind Henri, laughing and singing. Sometimes Nancy would be there too, all three of them riding together, with Lorenzo in the middle—rising and rocking to the rhythm of the ride.

But they could never let him go riding on his own. He wanted to, longed to, but they dared not let him—he could not balance well enough. He had tried, often, but had always fallen off. It angered him and frustrated him, and when he was like that he would start to shout, to hit his head with his hands, and storm about the place, in a fit of rage, sometimes for hours on end before he calmed down.

There was one horse, though, that he discovered he could ride. This is where I come into the story, and how I first met Lorenzo. **"**

CHAPTER 7

The Charbonneau Carousel

"Lorenzo and I first saw one another on a spring morning forty years ago. It was market day in the town square in Aigues-Mortes, and holiday time for the children in town. Maman and Papa and I, we had spent all the day before setting up our beautiful carousel, the carousel that Papa had made with his own hands. He had carved all the animal rides himself, and Maman had painted them in bright colors, all the colors of the rainbow. Papa was very proud of it, so was she, and so was I, and so were all our Roma family.

We always caused quite a stir wherever and whenever we arrived, our carousel in bits and pieces, piled up into carts behind us. Family and friends would all come along to help put it up. It is what we always did during the spring and summer months, Vincent. We traveled the countryside with our carousel. We would set up in a village maybe, or in a field on the edge of a town, anywhere they would let us. We were quite a tradition, I can tell you. Remember, Vincent, this was a very long time ago. There was no television, of course, no films either, or very rarely. Just the Charbonneau Carousel. We were the big attraction.

But this was the first time we had ever brought the carousel to Aigues-Mortes. It was Papa's idea. It was the biggest town around, he said. Business would be good there, with plenty of customers, lots of children, who might come again and again to have a ride on the carousel. We could stay for awhile maybe. Maman liked the idea, as he knew she would. Roma families like us, traveling families, generally we like to keep moving on. But Maman always wanted to stay in a place longer than Papa. We Roma, Vincent, we have a saying. We like to follow the bend in the road, to be free to go where we want. "

*

My heart leaped. I hadn't told her my story of the old traveler and the policeman, and I so wanted her to know it now, that in a way it was following the bend in the road that had brought me here. But I did not dare interrupt her again. I would tell her later.

"So that's why we came to Aigues. We found a place for our caravan in a field down by the canal, just across the water from the town walls, where the horse had grass to graze, and water to drink. Honey, our horse was called. Unfortunately, I was the one who had to look after her, see she was fed and watered, pick out her hooves, groom her. Honey was not at all sweet. Badly named she was. *Très méchant, ce cheval!* She had a wicked temper. I never liked her and she never liked me. But for pulling the caravan she was the best horse we ever had.

They let us set up our carousel in the square, under the shade of a great plane tree, close to the church and the cafés and the shops, right in the heart of the town. It was a perfect pitch for the Charbonneau Carousel. The town was busy, the people seemed friendly, and, as Papa had said, there were lots of children about, so the rides on the carousel were almost always full. On fine days, when the wind was not blowing, and the rain was not driving in, we did good business.

We stayed there in Aigues-Mortes, of course, to earn money—everyone has to do that, Vincent, as I am sure you know. But there was another reason why Maman in particular was happy to stay put in one place much longer than usual, as I was soon to discover. Now that I was older— Maman broke the news to me soon after we arrived in Aigues—she told me we would be staying in the town long enough for me to be able to go to school for awhile, to learn to read and write. And Aigues, she said, seemed the perfect place for me to start school. I never liked the idea at all. But Maman was very determined. So on weekdays I found myself, like it or not, going off to school, along with all the other children in town. But more about school later.

After school, and at the weekends, I was still where I most wanted to be, working on the carousel in the town square with Maman and Papa. Papa turned the handle to make it go round. He was as strong as an ox, shoulders and arms as hard as wood. Maman took the money and played the barrel organ, and I helped the children up, and looked after them once the carousel was turning, making sure they did not fall off nor try to jump off while it was turning. But, best of all, I was the one who had to bring in the customers, tempt them in, and I had my own special way of doing it.

I always chose Horse to ride, because he was the most popular. I would jump up onto his back, and, with the carousel turning, I would shout it out all over the square. "Roll up, roll up for the Charbonneau Carousel! Come along, come along! Have the ride of your life: on Lion, or Tiger, on Elephant, or Dragon, or Bull, or on Horse, this lovely white horse from the Camargue! Roll up, roll up!"

Then Maman would play her barrel organ for awhile to entice everyone in, and I would go on with my shouting. I would hang on to the pole, one-handed, swinging myself out, as Papa turned the carousel round and round. I would leap from ride to ride, whooping with joy, showing the whole town how much fun it was. I loved to show off. I could put on quite a performance, Vincent—you should have seen me! We were a good team, Maman, Papa, and me. Some days it could be slow, but most days, especially on market days and weekends, we would soon have children queuing up for a ride, all of them impatient to have their turn, to be off.

In the darkening summer evenings, the carousel would be a blaze of color and lights—providing that Papa's generator worked. Sometimes it did; sometimes it didn't. It was—how do you say this?—a bit temperamental, that machine. Everyone in the town loved hearing Maman's barrel organ and watching the carousel going round. In the spring and summer of every year, the Charbonneau family carousel was the heart and soul of Aigues-Mortes, and that made me very proud.

But, much as the townspeople might have loved the bright lights and music and the fun of our carousel, there were a few who did not like us, who shunned us in the street. I was still young, and I could not understand why. It upset me greatly, and made me angry too. Maman told me to pay no attention, that this was just how some people were, and that I would have to get used to it, that there were kind people in this world, and nasty people. That was just how it was. But I never really understood any of this properly, not until I went to school. 〞

CHAPTER 8

Rousel Rousel!

"I never wore shoes in the summer, as all the other children did. And the clothes that Maman had made for me—the long red skirt I always wore—did not look like anything they wore. And I had long, straggly dark hair down to my shoulders. My hair did not look like their hair. Some of them would sneer at me, and say how poor I must be to live in a caravan and not in a proper house. Soon enough, though, I realized there was more to it than that. There were other reasons, deeper reasons, I discovered, for their hostility. I was Roma, a "gypsy," to them. I was "gyppo girl." I looked different. I had darker skin than most of them—and that was true, of course—but they said I was dirty, which I was not. It was also because I could not read or write as they could—which was true as well. That, after all, was why Maman had sent me to school.

Some of them just avoided me, looked the other way, or walked off. I could tell also that they were nervous of me, and I did not understand why they should be. I mean it was true that if someone taunted me, if someone picked a fight—boy or girl—I always fought back and I always won. I was good at fighting. Winning was my way to survive in that school, whether in fights or in races. I found I could run faster, jump farther, stand on my hands for longer than anyone else, do somersaults and backflips better than any of them. But none of that helped me to make friends.

There were some children—and a few teachers too, sad to say—who made it quite clear they did not like having me in their school, or even in their town. When I told Papa and Maman about all this, both of them told me to be proud and ignore them. But it was hard for me to realize that so many of those children who loved riding on our carousel, whom I had often helped climb up onto Tiger or Horse or Elephant, had in fact despised me all along, and not just me, but Maman and Papa too, all Roma people like us.

I was glad we lived away from them, in our caravan outside the town walls, on the other side of the canal. But I never minded at all being in the town square, working on the carousel. I was so proud of it, of Maman and Papa, and anyway I loved the bustle of the place. I did miss my Roma friends and family, though. I was away from my cousins, who were really my only friends, with whom we so often traveled during the rest of the year. Until the day I met Lorenzo, I had no one in that town I could really call a friend.

As I said, it was on a market day in spring in the school holidays that Lorenzo first came into my life. The carousel was turning, the music was playing, the rides were full of laughing children, all enjoying themselves. I was enjoying myself—everyone was. I noticed then a boy jumping up and down on the far side of the square. Even far away, I could see he was in a state of high excitement, waving his arms and clapping with joy at the sight of the carousel. Then he was taking his mother's hand and dragging her toward us. I was used to seeing children come skipping up to the carousel, begging to be allowed to have a ride. The music drew them in—like moths to a flame, Papa always said—and I could see that this particular moth, this clapping boy, was fluttering with frantic excitement. The next time I came round on the carousel, he was still standing there, watching as the ride slowed down, calmer now, waiting, waiting, as children often did for their favorite animal ride to come by.

But, when the carousel came to a stop, I could see he was not looking at all at Elephant or Dragon, or Bull or Horse; instead, he was gazing higher up, mouth open in wonder, at the dozens of flying pink flamingos that Papa had carved, and Maman had painted, which made up the frieze that crowned our carousel.

"Flam flam! Flam flam!" he cried, pointing up at the flamingos, clapping his hands and bouncing up and down, quite unable to contain his excitement. Some people were laughing at him, but he didn't notice. He had eyes only for the flamingos. Other children were already climbing up on the carousel by now, choosing their animal for the next ride, and I was helping them up one by one, looking after them as best I could, telling them as usual to hold on tight, not to get off while the carousel was turning.

By the time I had finished doing all that, I could see this boy was becoming quite agitated. His mother was trying to encourage him to go for a ride on Horse, but he kept shaking his head and pulling away. "I can't understand it," the mother was calling up to me. "Lorenzo wants to get on—I know he does. He loves horses, but he loves those flamingos up there more."

The boy was looking at me now and—don't ask me how—I knew at once what he was thinking. I said to him: "Flamingos need to fly free, don't they? You can't ride them. They would not like it. But you could ride Horse. He would love you to ride him." I was standing right beside Horse, patting the saddle, inviting him up. "He's a kind horse, never bites or kicks, I promise. We could ride him together, if you like."

He was unsure. He was still thinking about it. I held out my hand. After some moments of hesitation, and a nervous look back at his mother for reassurance, he reached up and took my hand. I helped him up, and settled him on Horse, showed him how to hold on to the pole in front of him with both hands. I mounted up behind him, and put my hands on his shoulders. By now, he was bouncing up and down in the saddle, longing to get going.

"He won't fall off, will he?" his mother asked me. "You will look after him?"

"I will stay with him," I told her. He turned to me then and gave me such an openhearted smile, a smile of complete trust. I have never forgotten the warmth of that first smile.

"Renzo," he said, tapping his head. "Renzo."

Then he tapped mine. "Kezia," I told him.

"Zia Zia," he said. And that is what he has called me ever since.

I waved my hand high in the air, the signal for Maman and Papa to begin the ride, that everyone was settled and ready to go. She started up the music on the barrel organ—the first tune was always "Sur le Pont d'Avignon"—and then we were moving, turning.

I had one hand on Renzo's arm now to reassure him. I felt his whole body tense, heard a sharp intake of breath, saw the white of his knuckles as he gripped the pole with both hands. He was letting out loud shrieks of alarm and excitement. After just one turn of the carousel, these shrieks had turned to peals of ecstatic laughter, screeches of joy. Within a few minutes, he was daring to hold on to the pole with only one hand, and was waving to his mother. He was not just sitting on Horse now, he was riding him, rising to the movement, and loving every moment of it. His mother was too. Every time we passed by her, she seemed to be enjoying it as much as he was, laughing with him.

"Val Val!" he called out to her.

"Val Val!" she echoed. I had no idea what they were saying. They had their own language, those two.

Then, all too soon, it was over and they were walking away under the trees, back toward the market stalls. He kept looking over his shoulder at me, skipping along beside his mother, hopping with happiness. I hoped that he would be back, that at last I might have made a real friend in this place. But then he was lost in the crowd around the market stalls and was gone. I looked for him day after day, after that first meeting on the carousel, but he did not come back. 〞

CHAPTER 9

Fly, Flamingo, Fly

"I was never more miserable than in the days that followed. At school, our teacher, Monsieur Bonnet—I still hate the sound of his name—was picking on me and punishing me continuously. He kept telling me in front of the whole class that I was an ignorant child, a stupid gypsy child, a wicked heathen child. In the playground, some of the children in my class—Joseph and Bernadette were always the ringleaders—began to gang up on me. They told me to my face that they had decided from now on that no one would speak to me, because I was a "gyppo girl," who dressed in rags, they said, who couldn't even read. They did not speak to "dirty gyppos," they said. Joseph would grab at my skirt, and Bernadette would pull my hair!

There was only one teacher I liked, Madame Salomon. She would come over and talk to me sometimes when no one else would. She wasn't my class teacher, but I wished she was. But then one day Monsieur Bonnet told us that Madame Salomon had left the school and would not be coming back. "A good thing too," he said. "We don't need her kind here." I had no idea what he meant. Not then.

I ended every day at that school feeling I was utterly alone in the world. I begged Maman and Papa to let me stay home with them, to help them every day on the carousel, like I did in the evenings and at the weekends, but they were adamant. They had never learned to read or write, or to do their sums, they said, but the world was changing. Everyone needed school these days. The old ways were going, like it or not. Roma children had to learn just like other children, or else everyone would think we were ignorant. I had to go to school: that was all there was to it. I argued, I cried, I threw tantrums. Nothing would change their minds.

But then one day Monsieur Bonnet lost his temper with

me, worse than he ever had before. It was probably my fault. I had a way of looking at him I knew he hated. I would glare at him, my eyes full of insolence and defiance.

He yelled at me in front of everyone in the playground. "We don't like you at this school! We don't like you gypsies round here!" So I lost my temper too, and told him just what I thought of him, that I didn't like him or his stupid school either. Seething with anger, he came over to me, and slapped me across the face.

That was it. I ran off out of the playground, out of the school, promising myself I would never go back. Even then, Maman and Papa tried to change my mind. Time and again, Maman took me to the school gates, day after day for a week, and made me walk in, which I did. But I stayed only for a few minutes, then climbed back over the gate, and ran home. Nothing they said, or the teachers could say or do, would make me stay there a day longer. I had my way in the end. Maman and Papa gave up. I was back where I wanted to be, working with them full-time on the carousel.

So I was there a couple of weeks later, on market day

again, when I saw Lorenzo come running across the square toward us.

"Flam flam! Rousel!" he was calling. "Rousel! Zia Zia!"

His mother was trying to hold him back, but he broke free of her, and came running up to the carousel. I gave him a hand and helped him up. He went straight to Horse, swung his leg over and got on by himself, much to my surprise. He grasped the pole and began bouncing up and down, raring to go, willing the carousel to get moving. But Papa never liked to begin turning the carousel until we had as many children as possible mounted up and ready to ride.

"Val Val, Val Val!" Lorenzo was shouting again and again. I still had no idea what he meant.

His mother, who had arrived breathless by now, was trying to tell me. "*Cheval*," she explained. "He means '*cheval*.' He likes to say bits of words for some reason. He doesn't speak whole words very often. Just bits of words, don't you, Renzo? 'Renzo' is for 'Lorenzo,' 'rousel' for 'carousel,' and 'val' for '*cheval*.' 'Rousel' has been his favorite word all week. He loves your carousel, talks about it all the time, about the horse, about those flying pink flamingos up there. He loves flamingos. And he talks about you. He calls you Zia Zia. You have been very kind to him."

"He has been very kind to me," I told her as the carousel began to turn, and the barrel-organ music filled the square. Round we went, Lorenzo abandoning himself to his laughter. Every time we came round again now, I saw his mother and Maman talking together beside the barrel organ. I had a feeling even then that they were hatching something, but had no idea what it might be. I could see they were enjoying watching us both.

So I was not taken entirely by surprise when Maman told me that evening what she had in mind. I was sitting on the edge of the canal with Papa, dangling a line, hoping for a fish. She came to sit beside us. "I was talking to Madame Sully, Lorenzo's mother, your friend's mother," she began. "Papa thinks it's a good idea too, don't you, Papa?" Papa nodded, and shrugged, which was always his way of half agreeing with Maman.

"What's a good idea?" I asked, not really listening.

"Well, I told her about school, about you not liking it, not going there anymore," Maman went on. "It was her idea, not mine. She told me she'd be more than happy to give you some lessons, in reading, writing, and mathematics. She was a teacher once, you know, before she married. She'd like to do it. So we made a deal. You know how I like to do deals! I said that maybe we could give Lorenzo lots of free rides on the carousel whenever they come to town on market days, and in exchange you could go out to their farm once a week for your lessons. It's not far. Papa said he would mend the tires on the bicycle for you, didn't you, Papa? What d'you think? **"**

And there the story stopped for a few moments as Kezia leaned forward and threw another log on the fire. I thought for a moment she might not continue. But, much to my relief, she went on.

"So now you know, Vincent. That's how it happened. I first came to the farm, to this house, forty years ago now. I cycled out here once a week—it took me no more than thirty minutes or so to get here. I'd sit down in this room with Madame Sully, Lorenzo's mother, and have my lessons. And every week, on market days, Lorenzo would come into town for his ride on the carousel, all the rides he wanted. I think each of us looked forward to those days as much as the other.

It is maybe difficult for you to believe, Vincent, but I had never in my life been in a proper house before, one that was not pulled by a bad-tempered horse called Honey, never been in a house that did not shake in the mistral, that did not move on wheels. And Madame Sully, my new teacher, was as unlike the horrible Monsieur Bonnet at school as it was possible to be. She was the best teacher anyone could have, as kind to me as Madame Salomon had been. She made lessons fun. She was strict with me, though. She expected me to concentrate, to do my work, but she was always friendly and fair. There was no fear anymore in my lessons, as there had been with Monsieur Bonnet.

Even so, I found it hard to learn sometimes. My concentration was not good. The older you are, Vincent, the harder it is to learn. But Nancy—after awhile, she did not like me to call her Madame Sully—was endlessly patient with me, always encouraging. I could do mathematics easily enough, but reading, and especially writing, I found hard. She would always end each lesson by reading me a story from one of the books on her shelf. And I looked forward to that every time.

I had always loved listening to stories. But, before this, no one had ever read to me from a real book. Maman and Papa had told them often, stories they knew, stories they made up. Every animal on the carousel had a story. There were stories about the places we had traveled, lots of stories of saints—especially about Saint Sarah, my favorite saint, the patron saint of gypsies, you know—and there were stories of pirates too, and of knights and dragons. But Nancy read her stories from a book, stories made by words on a page, written-down words that came to life when they were read out loud. It was all a new magic to me. Learning to read the words made proper sense to me now. After every lesson, Nancy would give me a book to take home so that I could practice my reading.

But I was never so keen to practice my writing. She always gave me copying to do for my homework, and this did not come easily to me. Maman tried to make me do it at home, in the caravan, but I never liked it. I preferred to be outside, working on the carousel in the town square, or going fishing with Papa, or even looking after horrible Honey. Usually, I put off doing my copying until the day before my next lesson with Nancy out at the farm. I think I only ever did it then because I did not want to upset her.

I so looked forward to those lesson days, loved arriving at the farm out on the marshes, because Lorenzo would always be waiting for me. He would come running down the farm track when he saw me, to escort me to the farmhouse, honking his flamingo greeting, arms outstretched in welcome. But after that, during my lessons, I would not see much of him. Sometimes I did catch glimpses of him riding out over the farm up behind Henri, on their horse, Cheval, herding sheep, or the black bulls, or the herd of white horses, or he'd be out in the farmyard, feeding the hens. He was always busy outside and I was busy inside.

He came into the house for lunch with Henri, but he never sat down. He ate on the move, grazing, usually sausage and sometimes cheese—sausage was his favorite even then, Vincent. There was always a restlessness about him. One moment he was a honking flamingo, wheeling about the room. But, in a trice, he could turn from flying flamingo to hopping frog to galloping horse, with sound and voice to match, and match perfectly too. He was never doing it to show off either. He became these creatures, inhabited their whole being. It wasn't a game. Whatever creature he became at any moment was part of who he was.

I had been coming out to the farm for my lessons with Nancy for awhile by now, and with every visit I was made to feel more and more at home, as if I was one of the family. Lorenzo was already treating me like a sister. There was trust and friendship between us. So when in the middle of lunch one day he grasped me by the hand, made me get up from the table and follow him outside, I went along willingly. I could feel it was important to him that I did. He held my hand all the way across the yard, and led me toward a long shed behind the barn. Outside the door he turned to me and put his finger to his lips.

Coming out of the sunlight into the darkness, I found it difficult to see at first. I could make out pens in the corner, a couple of sheep in one, a black cow and calf in another, and there was a white horse, an old Camargue horse, lying down on his own in another corner. As we approached, the horse got up, shook himself, snorted, then bowed his neck to be stroked. And, all the while, Lorenzo was talking to him, not in words, or even bits of words, but as a horse talks—"horse murmuring" you might call it. He did much the same then with the cow that was lying down in the corner, the calf beside her. He crouched down, and put his forehead on hers. When he murmured now, it was the murmur of a contented cow. He climbed over into the sheep pen and lay down amongst them, humming to them. He wanted me to join him. So I did. They gathered around us, nuzzling us, bleating softly, talking to us.

I looked up some time later to see both Nancy and Henri standing there, watching us.

"Lorenzo cures animals. He has a gift," Nancy told me. "These animals are not always ours. These sheep are, but that horse isn't. Sometimes neighboring farmers bring their animals to us, because they know Lorenzo can cure them. Don't ask me how. He just can. He talks to them—and not just farm animals either, wild animals too—frogs, birds, beetles, terrapins, flamingos. He puts his hands on them, breathes on them, and they get better. Not always, of course, but often."

Lorenzo was climbing now into another pen in the darkest corner of the shed. Something stirred as he went down on his knees in the straw and crawled toward it. Then it rose up on trembling legs, stood there unsteadily, and cheeped—a fledgling flamingo.

Coming out of the shed that day, Lorenzo spread his wings and ran around the farmyard in the sunshine, honking happily. Then he came to me, lifted my arms, held them out wide, and beat them up and down. He was making wings of my arms. I knew at once what he wanted me to do. I became a flamingo too, wings wide outstretched as his were, honking as he was, flying as he was. No play-making this, no make-believe. I was a flamingo. I ran like a flamingo. I lifted off and flew away after Lorenzo.

"Fly, flamingo, fly!" Nancy cried. "Bravo, Renzo! Bravo, Zia!" 〞

CHAPTER 10

We Live for That

"Nancy told me one day as I was leaving that I could come to the farm not just one day a week, but whenever I felt like it.

"More lessons would be good for you anyway—especially writing lessons. You certainly need them! And, which is more important, Lorenzo loves to be with you," she said. "You make him happy. Henri and me, we love to see him happy. We live for that."

So that's what I did. I went out to the farm whenever I could. Maman didn't mind because she thought it would be good for my schooling, and it was too. I loved it, because Nancy read to me after my lessons, especially if my writing had been good—King Arthur stories mostly, because, she said, Lorenzo always liked them best, so she thought I might too. And, soon enough, I found I was confident enough to try to read one of the Arthur stories aloud to her. I stumbled over some of the difficult words, but I did it. She was as proud of me as I was of myself.

But most of the time, though, I was outside with Lorenzo, either in his hospital shed, helping to look after the animals, or riding out with him and Henri across the farm. And Lorenzo would take me to sit with him on the upturned rowing boat by the pink lake. He loved that place. We would sit side by side and talk, or not talk. Mostly we would not talk, but watch the flamingos out on the island where they gathered and nested. And sometimes Henri would row us out there in the boat. Lorenzo was always counting them—it was to be sure they were all there, Henri said.

Lorenzo loved to count; he still does. In the blink of an eye, he would know how many flamingos were out on the island, if any were missing. He would check them, rescue any fledgling that seemed lost or weak or abandoned, and bring it to the shed to look after it, then, once it was strong again, he would take it back to the island.

I did notice, on my now frequent visits to the farm, that Henri and Nancy were always anxious to know where Lorenzo was. They told me to keep him in sight if possible, which was not at all easy because he did like to wander off sometimes on his own. Nancy told me once that one of the reasons they liked it so much when I came out to the farm was that they knew that if he did wander off any time he would as likely as not be with me, so they need not worry so much. It wasn't that he would get lost, Nancy said. He knew the farm as well as they did. But he did have moods sometimes, when something had upset him, and then he could become confused and agitated, so it was always better for someone to be with him, and keep him in sight at least.

They were worried too that he could not swim. The trouble was, they told me, that he did not seem to know it. If he saw a fledgling flamingo in the water that needed rescuing, he would just jump into the lake and do it—however deep the water was. Mostly the lakes were shallow, but in places they were deep enough to drown in, and so were the canals. So long as I was there to keep an eye on him—and Maman had told them how well I could swim—then they were happy.

Time and again, Lorenzo would try to find a way of postponing my leaving at the end of the day, if he could. One evening, as I was about to go home, he grabbed my hand and insisted on coming with me. "Lot, Zia," he was saying. "Lot Lot Lot."

Nancy laughed at this. "Well, you are honored, Kezia," she said. "Lot is Lorenzo's place, his special place. I am not allowed there without him, nor is his *papa* either."

Lorenzo held my hand tight—I could not have broken away even if I had wanted to. And I most certainly did not want to. His excitement was infectious. I wanted to know where this "Lot Lot" place was, and what it was; and when I found out I was amazed.

We were walking hand in hand down the farm track—the way I cycled home—when, without any warning, he suddenly dragged me off the track. We were walking through head-high reeds and rushes, then climbing a rutty hill, and onto a rickety wooden bridge. There below us now was a ditch, with a stream running through, and beyond the bridge I could see a ruin—it looked like the remains of an old castle or fort maybe, its stone walls rising from the reeds.

"Lot Lot!" Lorenzo cried, rushing me over the bridge and in under a great stone archway.

I found myself standing in a grassy courtyard, surrounded by the ruins of old castle walls, a huge stone rising in the middle. He let my hand go then, and, clapping his hands, he began telling me all about the castle—that was what I supposed he was talking about. He was waving his hands about, swishing and slashing and stabbing with a stick he had picked up, strutting about like some king, and tapping the side of his head.

"Art Art! Lot Lot!" He was shouting at me, face close to mine, hands on my shoulders, willing me to understand. I didn't.

There was more play-acting to come. He clambered up onto the stone, and I could see he was pretending to pull something out of it, tugging, straining, heaving. Then it came to me: Excalibur! The sword in the stone! Nancy had read me the story. I had read it to her myself only the day before. Lorenzo was pulling the sword out of the stone! He was King Arthur—Art Art—and I was standing in his castle, his Camelot—Lot Lot. At last I understood, and I could see he was so pleased I did.

He was calm now, but still breathless with excitement, as he stood there, smiling down at me. "Guin," he said, bowing low to me. "Guin Guin."

Guinevere. I had been made queen of his Camelot. Now I knew what Nancy had meant. He had brought me to his special place and made me his queen. I felt so honored, so truly honored.

Nancy told me often how Lorenzo looked forward more than anything else now to his trips to town on market days. He loved his ride on Horse on the carousel, and the music of our barrel organ as well, especially "Sur le Pont d'Avignon," which he would sing and hum again and again, in a monotone as always. Lorenzo did not hum tunefully, but he had perfect rhythm. Above all, he loved to see me, Nancy told me. Whenever he arrived in the town square, he would always spread his wings and fly toward me.

Most people in town loved to see Flamingo Boy, as people called him, and they were mostly kind to him. But after school, or on school holidays, when there were children about, there were those who were mean, the same ones who had been mean to me when I went to school— Bernadette was the worst. I noticed them, heard their nasty jibes, but Lorenzo never did, or, if he did, he ignored them. He only noticed if they picked on me. And one afternoon they did.

I had taken Lorenzo down to our caravan where he often liked to come after he had been on the carousel. We were sitting, side by side, on the bank of the canal, fishing, with Honey grazing nearby, when a group of boys came along, Joseph amongst them, on their way home from school. They spotted us there and began to taunt us.

"Gyppo girl, gyppo! Gyppo girl and Flamingo Boy! Loony boy! Loony boy! Gyppo! Gyppo!"

They were coming closer. We both tried to ignore them and went on fishing. But then they began throwing stones at us, at Honey too. One of the stones hit me on my ear. I could feel the blood trickling. Lorenzo reached out and touched my neck. He looked down at the blood on his fingers, and then at me, his eyes full of bewilderment and hurt.

He did not hesitate. He was up on his feet, and walking toward the boys, just like one of the black bulls on the farm about to charge, his shoulders hunched, his head lowered. Then he did charge, bellowing like a bull. The boys stopped in their tracks, silenced and suddenly terrified. They took to their heels and ran for it. Lorenzo came back, sat down and went on fishing as if nothing had happened. But I had seen another side to Lorenzo I had not known was there, a side I never saw again until some two years later when German soldiers marched into the town, and our whole world changed. **"**

CHAPTER 11

Occupation

"The afternoon the German soldiers came was market day, the town square bustling with people, the carousel turning, the music playing. The stallholders were busy selling, Nancy and Henri amongst them, and Lorenzo was riding Horse as usual, loving every moment of it.

It will seem strange to you now perhaps, Vincent, that we were not expecting it. After all, our country had been attacked and invaded three years before. Even we children knew that. We had heard endless talk of the Occupation and the war—I remember seeing people crying in the streets when we heard about it—but I suppose it was of little interest to me at the time, because I could not see it. So I could not really understand it. It seemed to be something that had happened to other people and a long way away. My life had been little changed by it, if at all.

This was because, up to now, the Germans had occupied mostly the north of France. Here, down in the south, in the Camargue, we were in what was then called the Vichy Zone, the unoccupied part of France. Only the north of the country had seen German soldiers in the streets—the black-and-red swastika flags flying. So far as we were concerned in the Camargue, everything had gone on much the same as before. There was less food to go around, and many men had been taken away as prisoners of war, or rounded up to be sent to work in Germany. But we had seen no German uniforms in the streets, no tanks, no planes, no bombing, no shooting. There were rumors that a railway line and some trucks had been blown up not far away, I remember, but there was little talk of resistance.

So far as I could understand it, the war was over for us. We had lost, and everyone was upset. I understood that. And no one likes losing. But our French tricolor flag still flew on the *mairie*—the town hall you call it in English, I think—in the town square, the gendarmes walked the streets as usual. We celebrated the fourteenth of July, as we always had, sang "La Marseillaise," the town band playing, and there were fireworks in the evening over the town.

We were living in the Free Zone, we thought, the unoccupied zone. France was still France here, and French; the Camargue was still the Camargue, and French; Aigues-Mortes was still Aigues-Mortes, and French. The mosquitoes and the heat were here in the summer; the mistral wind roared and rattled the rest of the time. And I suppose, looking back now, our carousel was just part of the same normality, the same reality, the reality we all knew and accepted. The carousel went on turning day after day, and the seasons came and went. Life went on much as before.

So the shock of seeing a German scout car come driving into the town square that afternoon, officers in gray uniforms and peaked caps in the back, and German soldiers coming in behind them—trucks full of them, with their shining black helmets, and their rifles—silenced the town instantly. The carousel stopped turning. The music stopped playing.

The town looked on in disbelief. No one moved. No one spoke. The leaves on the plane trees in the square rustled in the wind, but that was the only sound you could hear. Even the pigeons on the church roof seemed to have stopped their cooing.

Outside the *mairie*, the soldiers jumped down from their trucks and lined up. An officer got out of the scout car, and stood there for long moments, straightening his jacket, surveying the silent square imperiously, before turning to climb the steps to the *mairie*, accompanied by several soldiers. The mayor, Monsieur Dubarry, came out to meet him and escorted him into the building. It felt to me as if the whole town was holding its breath. The soldiers stood now in ranks in the square, facing the sullen hostility of the townspeople.

I was so intent on the drama unfolding in front of me that I did not realize that Lorenzo was no longer up on Horse, no longer on the carousel, until I saw him barging his way through the crowd toward the soldiers. He walked straight up to the first soldier he came to and began to push at him, pushing him so hard that the soldier was sent staggering back, dropping his rifle.

There was a murmur of astonishment first and then some muted vocal support amongst the crowd. And I knew why that was too. Lorenzo, Flamingo Boy, was doing what everyone else there wanted to do, would have done, if any of us had had the courage. He was walking along the line now, pushing soldier after soldier, each one harder. People were laughing openly, and there was even some nervous giggling and clapping.

The soldier in charge seemed at first unsure of what to do, but now he went after Lorenzo, grabbed him by the arm and held him. Lorenzo pulled away, then turned and did just the same to him, pushing him, then pounding him with his fists. One of the soldiers raised his rifle then. He was pointing it straight at Lorenzo.

No one was clapping now. No one was laughing. Until that moment, I had stood there, watching, too stunned to move or to think. But now I was running across the square through the crowd.

"Don't shoot! Don't shoot!" I was yelling. "He does not mean it. I'll look after him. Don't shoot!"

I had reached Lorenzo by now. I put my hand on his

shoulder, and spoke to him as softly and as calmly as I could, which I knew by now was the only way to be with him when he was upset.

"Renzo," I said, "come away now. We'll go fishing, shall we? Fish, fish."

I felt his whole body relax under my hand. He was still breathing hard, though, still as agitated as I had ever seen him.

The soldier in charge was barking an order and the rifle was lowered. Then he turned his attention to us. As he came closer, I saw he was much taller than the other soldiers, his face weather-beaten, his skin wrinkled like the bark of a tree. He walked with a limp, using a stick. The closer he came the taller he seemed to be. He was towering over us.

Frightened though I was, I remember thinking his helmet looked ridiculous on him, comical almost, far too big for such a thin man. It sat on his head like a huge upturned saucepan. Thin he may have been, but he was a giant of a man and the anger in his eyes was not comical at all. There was a long silence.

"He did not mean it," I told him.

"Yes, he did," the soldier replied. He spoke to me severely, but not as angrily as I thought he would. "This boy, you must tell him that it is not allowed to attack German soldiers. He could be shot. You have to make him understand."

"I will," I said. "I will."

"You are this boy's sister, are you not?" He spoke French easily and quite well.

I was about to explain that Lorenzo was not my brother, that he was better than a brother, that he was my friend. I was still searching for the words to answer him when he answered his own question, assuming he was right.

"If you are his sister, then you should look after him. He must not do this, you understand? If there is a next time, it will be very serious . . ."

Then Nancy was at our side. With scarcely a glance at the soldier, she led us both away from him, back through the crowd toward the carousel. Maman was running toward us, Papa close behind, both frantic with anxiety.

We were standing there in the town square, arms still around one another, when we all became aware that the people in the crowd were looking not at us anymore, but up at the balcony of the *mairie*. The French tricolor that always hung there had gone. Instead, two German soldiers were unfurling another flag, a huge red Nazi banner, a black swastika in the center.

Shortly afterward, the officer and the soldiers came out of the *mairie*. The officer got in the car and was driven off; and the tall giant of a soldier was marching all the others away. The crowd broke up; the market stalls shut down; cafés and shops closed their doors. The square emptied.

By this time too, we were closing down the carousel. Nancy and Henri and Lorenzo stayed with us, helping to put up the shutters all around. We were almost the only people left in the square now. When we had finished, we all went back to our caravan by the canal, lit the lamp, closed the door behind us and shut ourselves in.

I remember thinking that after this nothing would ever be the same again. But I had another thought as we huddled there together in our caravan, that we were all in a way part of the same family now. We may not have known one another that well or for very long, but at that moment we all felt very together somehow, protective of one another, close.

Maman was fiercely determined nothing should change just because the Germans were in the town, that we should go on just the same.

"Otherwise they win," she said, struggling to hold back her tears, "and we must never let that happen. So, the carousel goes on turning; and, Kezia, you must go on with your lessons out at the farm. Is that all right, Nancy?" Nancy was still too upset to speak, but she nodded. "And as for Lorenzo," Maman went on, "wasn't he wonderful? Facing up to the soldiers like that! Flamingo Boy is the hero of the town, if you ask me!"

We all laughed, because we needed to, and Lorenzo clapped his hands, delighted we were laughing. He loves laughter, as you know already, Vincent. He loves people to be happy around him. "

CHAPTER 12

Be Proud and Carry On

"So, after the Germans came that day, I would cycle out to the farm just as I had before, as often as possible. Maman and Papa went every day to the square to open up the carousel, but very few people came now. Papa became very disconsolate at times, and kept saying we should take it down, pack up, and move on somewhere new. But Maman argued that it would be the same elsewhere, that the Germans were bound to be everywhere by now, that wherever we went we would not be able to escape them. She insisted that once people got used to having the Germans about—and they would—they would come out again to enjoy themselves. It was human nature, she said, for people to want to have fun, and that maybe they would need the carousel even more now, to raise spirits, to forget their troubles, the war and the Occupation. We had to be proud and carry on.

Every day, if the weather was fair, Maman and Papa would go to the town square, open up the carousel, play the barrel organ, and wait for the families and children to come. I loved to hear "Sur le Pont d'Avignon" echoing around the square. It was our song, a song all French people knew and loved. And that was important now, even to a child as young as I was. I understood what it meant. That song was part of who we were, and the Germans could not take it away from us.

Maman put up posters all over the town, and handed out dozens of leaflets telling everyone that it was half price now for a ride on the Charbonneau Carousel. Still people didn't come. In the town square now, there were always German soldiers to be seen, drinking in the cafés, strolling in the streets, wandering wherever they liked, chatting to anyone who would talk to them. They were making themselves at home. One or two even came to have a ride on the carousel, which only made Papa even more upset. He told them the carousel was for children, but they just laughed and got up onto it anyway. There was nothing he could do. I hated to see them there too, which was another reason why I was always more than happy to go off to the farm for my lessons, and to see Lorenzo. I longed for my lessons, and I longed even more to be with Lorenzo.

My lessons went on with Nancy right here in this room, sitting just where you are now, Vincent. I still enjoyed them, but I wanted more and more to be outside with Lorenzo. Nancy knew it, of course. She would see me looking longingly out of the window, and sometimes she would take pity on me and cut my lessons short. She would often send me on my way with her book of King Arthur stories.

"Go on, then, Kezia, go and read to him in his Camelot. It is good for your reading practice anyway," she would say. "He would love it if you read it to him there."

So that's what I often did. On the great stone in the courtyard of the ruined castle in the marshes, I would sit and read to Lorenzo. He liked it so much that he never wanted me to stop. I could see him mouthing every word as I read it, living the story in his head. Some of it he really did know word for word, and sometimes would even finish the sentence for me. The words might be garbled, abbreviated, but they were recognizable. He was telling me the story his way. We had magical times together in that place. I always hated to leave.

Every time I cycled home now, I knew I would find Papa ever more silent and somber in the caravan. I sensed also that Maman was tense, and not herself at all. She was nervous, frightened even, whenever she heard voices from across the canal or outside the caravan. She dodged my questions, and, however much I asked, would not tell me what it was that was troubling her. I thought it must be the Occupation, of course, the constant presence of the German soldiers in the town. As I was to discover later, it was much more than that.

So, over the days and weeks that followed, the caravan became an ever more sad and difficult place for me to come home to. Out on the farm, with my other family—as I had come to think of them by now—I felt free and happy, with no thought of the Occupation. I just wanted to stay there with Lorenzo in his Camelot for as long as I could, and so would try to find any excuse to put off cycling home until the last possible moment.

On the day it happened, there were gray clouds gathering over the marshes. I told Nancy that a storm was coming in from the sea and that I could be blown off my bike on the road home, that maybe I should wait awhile and not go home yet, not until the storm had passed. But Nancy knew my game. She said I was right, that there was a storm coming, which was all the more reason why I should go home now, before it got any worse. I never argued with Nancy—I never even tried. I liked her too much, and anyway I knew I would not win.

So, whether I wanted to or not, I had to go. As usual, Lorenzo walked me down the farm track a little way. We said good-bye, and he pushed me off on my bicycle as he always did, and ran along beside me till I was going too fast for him. It was the same every time.

Lorenzo loved everything to be the same, even good-byes. Good-byes, hellos, sausages, and songs, he loved what he knew, never wanted anything to be different. The trouble is that things do change, whether we like it or not. And for Lorenzo any change was always difficult. It still is sometimes.

A mistral wind is wild and unpredictable, Vincent, and treacherous too. There was a strong and gusting wind on the way back, but I had an easy enough ride along the canal, for awhile. The track is quite protected there. Then, quite suddenly, I found myself out of the shelter of the high rushes and on the open road, with nothing but wide lakes on either side of me, at the mercy of the sudden fury of a vicious gale that was roaring in over the marshes. There was no hiding place. I just had to put my head down and pedal hard. I cycled most of the way into a headwind so strong that time and again I was forced to get off and walk. The water in the lakes was being whipped up into white-capped waves—I had never seen it like that before.

Cycling became impossible. I had to walk the rest of the way. As I came over the bridge just outside the town walls, it was all I could do to keep upright in the wind. There was driving rain with it now that was stinging my eyes if ever I tried to lift my head.

I knew something was wrong as soon as I reached our

field. The door of the caravan was open and banging in the wind. Honey was in the field, but I could not see Maman and Papa anywhere. I called for them. No one answered. I looked inside the caravan. No one was there. So they had to be at the carousel in town. But in a storm like this no one would be on the rides. Maman and Papa would have shut it down by now. Maybe they were still busy doing it. It was the only place left I could think of to look for them.

I left my bicycle, and set off on foot, running. As I came into the town square, I saw at once what had happened. The great plane tree in the middle of the square had been uprooted, and had come crashing down right on top of our carousel. It lay there in pieces under the branches, crushed, flattened, destroyed. A huge crowd of people was gathered around, Maman and Papa amongst them. They were standing side by side, Maman's head on Papa's shoulder, looking down at the wreckage of their lives. "

CHAPTER 13

The Day the Music Died

"Standing there in the square with Maman and Papa, I could feel my whole being dissolve with sadness. Horse, Bull, Dragon, Elephant, all our rides, all our animals, lay there on the ground, broken and shattered.

Everyone was watching Papa now as he walked forward, brushing aside the leaves, stepping over the branches and the ruins of our carousel, and of Maman's barrel organ. Until then, I hadn't seen it lying there crushed, directly under the huge trunk of the tree, the generator beside it. Papa crouched down to pick up the remains of one of the flying pink flamingos. He stood up, piecing them together in his hands.

Then holding it high above his head, he said: "We will mend it." He repeated it, his voice full of fierce determination, shouting it out so that everyone should hear him against the roaring wind: "We will mend it!"

That was when I noticed some of the German soldiers standing there in amongst the crowd of onlookers, and I recognized the giant soldier. He was wearing a gray cap, not a helmet this time. His hair, I noticed, was snow white, which was strange for a man who was not that old. He was coming through the crowd toward us, and I was wondering why he limped, I remember. He stood there, tall and stiff, in front of Papa.

"They tell me you are Monsieur Charbonneau, the owner of this carousel." He spoke as stiffly as he stood. Papa did not reply. "Your papers? Identity papers?" the soldier demanded. Papa handed them over without a glance at him. "I have orders to clear all this away," the soldier went on. He handed the papers back.

"We shall do it ourselves," said Papa quietly.

"Very well, *monsieur*, as you wish." I thought that was all he was going to say. He noticed me then, standing beside

Papa, and I saw that he remembered me. "I wish to say, *monsieur*," he said, "that this was a very fine and beautiful carousel. I am sorry this happened."

"You do not need to apologize," Papa told him, but still not looking at him. "It was the mistral, the wind, that did this," Papa went on, "which is stronger than you are, stronger than all of us. You and your kind are to blame for much, but not for this, not for the mistral."

"I understand, *monsieur*," the soldier said. "But should you wish us to help you clear—"

"I thank you for your offer, but we can manage without your help," Papa told him coldly. And now he did look up at him, his face full of defiance. "If you really want to help, then perhaps you might take your soldiers and go back home where you belong."

The two men stood for some moments in silence, the giant soldier towering over Papa.

"Nonetheless," the soldier said, "I am sorry for your misfortune, *monsieur*." He smiled down at me then, and I found myself liking him, despite his uniform. I remember feeling a pang of shame that I liked him when I knew I should not, and all at the same time I was glowing with pride at how brave Papa had been to speak his mind.

Shortly afterward, the giant soldier led his men away, but most of the townspeople remained, unable to leave, still stunned at the destruction before their eyes, some of them crying openly, the older ones especially. I thought at the time, of course, that it was the destruction of the carousel they were sorrowing over, but I have realized since then that, for many there that day, the grieving must have been over the loss of the great plane tree, which had towered over their town, over their lives, and the lives of their forebears for hundreds of years, standing there as solid as the ancient church, and now so suddenly and cruelly struck down.

For many of the townspeople, the fall of that much-loved tree—so soon after the arrival of German occupiers—must have represented the ruination of everything that was precious to them, their town, their country, their liberty. The great tree was dead, but the leaves were still being blown about in great gusts, as if it was in its death throes.

To see old people in tears very nearly broke my resolve not to cry. But then, in just a few moments, all my sorrow was banished, and I was overwhelmed by a great and sudden gladness that held back my tears. Papa, Maman, and I found ourselves surrounded and comforted by the townspeople, men, women, and children—some of my worst school enemies amongst them. Monsieur Dubarry, the mayor, had his arm around Papa's shoulder. He, like so many, had rarely so much as deigned to speak to Roma people like us. But here they were, all gathering around us in our hour of need, voicing their opinions as to what should be done, and how. They were talking over one another so much that I could understand little of what they were saying or proposing, or what was going on. I knew only that somehow they were all intent on helping us recover what we could from this catastrophe.

Soon enough, the debate over, the square became a hive of activity. Horses and carts were sent for, axes and saws were fetched, and they all set to, hacking, chopping, sawing away at the crown of the tree, pulling aside the great branches that had crushed our beloved carousel. All this time, the rain lashed down and the wind raged around us. Tiles were blown off the rooftops and sent crashing to the ground; and those trees still standing in the square were being rocked and shaken above us with such violence that I was sure more of them must come down at any moment. But the towns-people seemed oblivious to all this. They worked on tirelessly. We all did, together.

Madame Salomon, my kind teacher from school, was there too, I noticed, a scarf covering her hair and head as if she did not wish to be seen. I wanted to run over and ask her why she had left the school, but she was too busy, and so was I. Our eyes met through the leaves of the fallen tree, and she smiled at me. When I looked up again, she was nowhere to be seen.

The more we pulled and cleared away the crown of the tree, the more we discovered that the damage done to the carousel was even worse than we had first supposed. Some of our animal rides were so broken up, so fragmented, that they were unrecognizable. As far as I could see, not a single one of the sixteen animals I knew and loved so well had survived intact, nor had the machinery that Papa main-tained meticulously so that every day it turned the carousel smoothly and regularly, at exactly five circuits a minute, no more, no less. It lay now battered and twisted under the debris of the tree. Papa bent down and retrieved his wooden cranking handle, and gave it to me for safekeeping. That at least was unbroken. He smiled for the first time then.

"Look after it, Kezia," he said. "We'll be needing it again."

By now, with the scale of the devastation evident before our eyes, we should have been in the depths of despair. But the recovery was already in full swing, everyone organizing everyone else, all of us retrieving what we could and, with the greatest of care, Maman, Papa, and I joining in the great rescue, gathering whatever we could. I picked up the head and broken horn of Bull, half the tail and a hoof of Horse, and the fractured leg of a flying pink flamingo.

By now, several carts were drawn up outside the church, horses pawing at the cobbles, heads tossing, impatient to be going. Soon a chain of townspeople was set up across the square and the remnants of the carousel were being passed from hand to hand, Papa and Maman supervising the loading of the carts outside the church. My chief tormentors at school, Joseph and Bernadette, were there in the chain, I saw, and many other children from school, all of whom had given me such a hard time, called me names, pulled my hair, thrown stones at me, spat at me even from across the street. When I smiled at them now, they smiled back, even Joseph, even Bernadette. I was amazed, and pleased, and angry all at the same time.

One by one, the carts would disappear and return awhile later to be filled again. So it went on, until every single piece of the carousel had been carried off. Maman, Papa, and I followed the last cart down the street, through the gateway under the town walls, over the canal, to our field, where Honey was grazing contentedly in the wind and rain, seemingly oblivious to us, to everything that had happened, and to the ruins of our beloved carousel that now lay all around her.

There it was, spread out on the grass in pieces, our precious carousel, like some enormous jigsaw puzzle emptied haphazardly out of the box and waiting to be put together. Some fragments had been deliberately gathered and arranged, so that a few of the animals were already a little more recognizable. I noticed at once that two of Dragon's legs and his tail were laid out together, and so was Elephant's head, one ear, and half of his trunk.

For some time, none of us spoke. Only then, I think, did I begin to take it all in, and the tears came at last, filling my eyes, running down my cheeks. I wiped them away, but Papa had already noticed. He put an arm round me.

"We are alone now, Kezia," he said. "You cry all you like. But always remember this: that everything happens for a reason, that beyond the clouds there is blue sky, beyond the sadness there is always joy. I mean we made friends today, did we not? And one day this carousel will turn again and the music will play and the children will come. It will happen. Maman and I, we made it once. We will make it again, and this time we have you to help us. You look after my cranking handle. I shall be needing it one day." I had never before heard Papa talk so passionately.

"Papa is right. What is broken can always be mended," Maman told me, stroking my hair and kissing the top of my head. "And the townspeople, they want it to be mended. You saw that they love the carousel, as we do. Why else did they bring all this here for us? We shall make it happen."

"But how?" I cried, the tears flowing freely now. "Look at it!"

As I spoke, I heard the honking of flamingos above us, and the singing of wings. I looked up to see a great flock of them overhead, hundreds of them, flying over the canal into the setting sun, and it was only then I thought of Lorenzo, and Horse, which he loved so much to ride. I could see now, in amongst the debris of the carousel, one of Horse's legs, and his battered head nearby. The rest of him was nowhere to be seen, lost amidst the wreckage. I knew then how devastated Lorenzo would be when he found out what had happened to the carousel, if he ever saw the remains of his beloved Val. It did not bear thinking about. **"**

CHAPTER 14

A New Dawn

"All night, as the storm blew itself out, I lay awake in the caravan, not so much grieving anymore over the carousel, but wondering how Lorenzo was going to react when he heard the news. Someone had to tell him that he would no longer be able to come for his rides on market days. Maman had already suggested that maybe it should be me that told him, because he knew me best, trusted me most, and that she would talk to Nancy about it in the morning. But how could I tell him Horse was broken, that his Val was in pieces? How could I tell him that? It would break his heart. I fell into a troubled sleep.

I was woken by voices outside the caravan. There was

no wind anymore, no rain pounding on the roof. I sat up in my bed. Maman and Papa were not in the caravan. Their bed was empty. Then I heard their voices outside, hushed, as if they did not want me to hear—and there were other voices too that I recognized. I looked out of the window. Nancy and Henri were out there with Maman and Papa, all of them in deep conversation. Then I saw Lorenzo. He was kneeling in amongst the remains of the carousel, rocking back and forth, cradling Horse's head on his lap, moaning softly over them, in a lullaby of grieving.

As I came down the steps, I called to him, but he did not turn, did not respond. Nancy came over and hugged me to her. "I am so sad for you," she said. "Lorenzo, as you see, is lost inside himself in his sadness, Kezia. He likes to be left alone when he is like this. Not like us. Sadness for us is often best shared, don't you think?"

I knew what she meant.

She talked on as she led me over toward Maman and Papa and Henri. "It's very strange, Kezia, but I think Lorenzo knew. I am sure of it. He knew something had happened. It was Lorenzo who made us come here this morning. All night, he was talking to himself, walking up and down, becoming more and more agitated. And it wasn't just the storm. He would not lie down and go to sleep. He was repeating it over and over again: 'Val Val Val. Zia Zia.' He kept taking us by the hand, tugging at us, trying all he could to make us get up. If we ever closed our eyes and tried to sleep, he would open our eyelids and peer in. He would not leave us alone until we got up. He took us outside to the barn and climbed up on to the cart. 'Val Val!' he was telling us. 'Zia Zia!' He was making it quite obvious what he wanted us to do. We had to go to town to see Val, to see you. We had no idea why, but he would not be put off. So we came. He knew what had happened, not exactly, of course. I am sure he sensed that his Val was in some danger, and that you were too."

"Morning, sleepyhead," said Papa, reaching for my hand. "You want to know what our friends here, Henri and Nancy, have offered us? They've said we can gather everything up, load the lot onto their farm cart. Four trips back and forth we think should do it. They've said we can take it all to the farm. They have a barn where we can store everything. It will be out of the weather. We can repair the carousel there, begin to put it all back together again. What do you think of that, Kezia? What friends they are to us!"

"And there is something else, Kezia," said Maman, "and you don't have to do it. But it was Nancy's idea. Tell her, Nancy. You should tell her."

"Well," Nancy began hesitantly, "we have all been thinking, Kezia. We thought you might like to bring the caravan and live out on the farm for awhile maybe, away from the town, while the carousel is being put together again. We could go on with your lessons. But we do have another reason for suggesting this, Kezia. Lorenzo will not have the carousel to ride on each week now, and he will miss that so much, and he will miss you. And, if I am honest, Henri and I, we should like the company of your *papa* and *maman* too. They have kindly said they would help out on the farm, and on a farm another pair of hands is always welcome. And, of course, there is the carousel. It may take months, maybe years, by the look of it, to put it to rights. But, if we are all there, we can all lend a hand, can't we? What do you think?"

I had a strong feeling even then that they were all holding something back from me, that this was not the whole story. Lorenzo, I saw, was still rocking back and forth in amongst the remnants of the carousel, still mourning his Val.

"What about Lorenzo?" I asked Nancy. "He likes things to be the same. You often tell me he does not like change. Maybe it will upset him to have us staying so close by all the time."

Nancy said: "Then you'd better ask him yourself, Kezia."

So I did. I went and knelt down beside him in amongst the debris. I stroked Horse's battered head and I asked Lorenzo whether he would mind if we came with our caravan to live on the farm for awhile, and we could all mend the carousel together. As I spoke, he stopped moaning, stopped rocking, and listened. He thought about it for awhile, then he handed me Horse's head to hold, folding my arms around it so that I would cradle it properly, the way he had.

"Zia Zia," he said. That was all he said, but it was enough. **"**

*

Kezia sat back and was silent for awhile. "When I talk about it, like this, it all seems like yesterday," she said. Then she turned to me with a smile. "And that, Vincent," she went on, "is how it was that we all came to live in our caravan here at the farm, how Papa and Maman lived and worked alongside Henri and Nancy, how I had my lessons every day, and how Lorenzo and I became even more like brother and sister, which is how we have stayed all these years."

It sounded like the end of her story.

"All's well that ends well, then," I said.

"How I wish that were true," she replied sadly. "Happy ever after happens only rarely in real life. I will tell you more another time, Vincent. It is late. I am tired now."

So she went up to bed and left me lying on the couch by the fire, hearing the music of the barrel organ in my head, seeing the carousel going around and around, and Lorenzo clapping his hands with wild delight, and the great tree crashing down, and the flock of flamingos flying overhead. I fell asleep to the sound of their honking, of their wings singing in the air.

CHAPTER 15

Not in Front of Lorenzo

I was getting better all the time, but it was a slow and unpredictable recovery. There were days when I woke up and was sure I was completely well, but then an hour or two later my head would be throbbing again. I was no longer feverish, but if I tried to get up and walk about I would feel weak all over. I still slept a lot too. And, when I woke, Lorenzo would often be there, sitting on a chair beside me, holding my hand. Seeing my eyes open, he would be on his feet at once, clapping his hands with excitement, calling for Kezia, and she would be there soon enough with a bowl of yogurt and honey, or steaming soup, or cheese, or sausage, which Lorenzo would always pinch off my plate. He thought that was very funny, and I didn't mind. I didn't much like that kind of sausage anyway—it wasn't like the sausage at home. To be honest, I preferred Watford sausage to Camargue sausage.

They were both always delighted to see me eating so well. And it was true that my appetite and my energy were improving with every day. Lorenzo, I could see, was longing to take me out, often leading me determinedly toward the door, but Kezia was always there to stop him.

"Later, Renzo," she would say. "Later. Soon. When he is stronger, you can take him outside. For now, he must stay inside, stay by the fire."

My schoolboy French was just about good enough to understand what she was telling him. I had noticed already that Kezia never told him not to do something if he really wanted to do it. She would simply suggest another idea he might like instead, often handing me the King Arthur book to read to him, which he rarely refused. It was in French, of course, which I read with my horrible French accent, and that made him laugh a lot.

So for the moment my horizons were still limited to my

couch by the fire, and to the one room with the photographs everywhere on the walls. I had the daily lives of Lorenzo and Kezia going on all around me, and Ami sleeping at my feet, or with his nose in the fire almost. Ami was a sweet-natured dog, though not beautiful, that's for sure. He did rather smell too, especially when he had been out in the rain and was drying off. In all three, I had the best of companions. I had never felt more at home, not even back in Watford, and that seemed a whole world away to me now.

It had been a few days since Kezia had told me her story. She had said there was more to come, and I was impatient to know what had happened to everyone. I did venture to ask her once whether they ever did manage to rebuild the carousel. It was a clumsy attempt to remind her, to prompt her, into continuing her story. Lorenzo was in the room at the time, standing at the window, watching for flamingos as he so often was. Kezia's frown was enough to warn me that this was not the right moment. But Lorenzo had heard me asking about the carousel, and became suddenly and inexplicably agitated. Kezia went to stand with him for awhile by the window, her arm around him.

"Look, Renzo. Grette grette," she said, pointing.

"Grette grette," he echoed. "Grette grette. Capo Capo." And then suddenly his mood changed and he was clapping his hands, and laughing. "Flam flam!" he cried. "Flam flam!" He was happy again.

As Kezia came by me, she bent down, hand on my shoulder. "Not in front of Lorenzo," she whispered. "There are things that happened when he was little that he does not like to remember. He remembers, but he does not want to be reminded. He understands everything, remembers everything better than we imagine, better than I do, I think. He feels everything deeply. When Lorenzo is happy, then all is well in the world. But anything that upsets him, anything that worries him, like a bad memory—and just a word sometimes is enough to set him off—then he slips so easily, so quickly, into sadness and despair. Maybe this evening, after he has gone to bed. Maybe I will tell you more then."

That evening, Lorenzo seemed to take forever to get himself off to bed, almost as if he knew he would be missing something if he went upstairs, as if he understood full well

I wanted him out of the room so that I could hear the rest of Kezia's story.

Kezia waited till we could hear him climbing into his squeaky bed upstairs. "He'll hum himself to sleep for awhile, then we will hear him snoring," she said, smiling. She was leaning forward now, speaking low. "We do not talk much about those times, Lorenzo and I, because it makes us both sad. He hates to see me sad and I hate to see him sad. But, without him here, it is good for me to talk about these things, Vincent, to think about those days, because, in amongst the sad times, we had such good times too. I like to remember the people, all those faces in the photographs on the walls. I like to talk about them—it brings them to life for me. So I am glad you are here, Vincent, glad to tell you, glad and sad."

She hesitated then, looking at me thoughtfully, before going on. "I was just thinking how strange it is. I have told this story to only one other person, and he was English too—older than you, but English. Strange." She sat back in her chair, listening as the humming upstairs finally subsided, and then stopped. We heard regular breathing, then snoring. She smiled. "*Voilà*," she said. "*Il dort*. He's asleep. *Alors*, where was I?"

"You had come to live on the farm with your *maman* and *papa*, in your caravan," I told her.

"Ah yes, *c'est vrai*, that's right, after the storm, after the tree came down. But there is something I did not tell you. For reasons I did not understand at the time at all, we loaded up the remains of the carousel at night, and made the journey to the farm in the caravan in the darkness, Nancy and Henri leading in two farm carts piled high with all that was left of our precious carousel. Maman took me aside and said I mustn't make a noise or talk, that it was better if no one knew where we were going. But she would not tell me why, no matter how much I asked.

All I understood was that we must be running away from some unspoken danger. I felt as if we were going into hiding, that in the town there was danger, that we would be safer out on the farm with the Sully family. Maman and Papa never went back into Aigues-Mortes after we left, not once. No one would explain to me why not.

We would hear how things were changing in town since the Occupation from Henri and Nancy when they came back once a week from market. They told us just how grim and sad a place Aigues had become. Until then, everything might have seemed to be much as before, the children going to school in the morning, the shops and cafés open, the church bell ringing. But now there were always German soldiers in the streets, an ever-present reminder that the world had changed. Worse even than the soldiers, they said, were the feared and detested brown-shirted police they called the Milice. I did not yet understand who they really were or what they did, except that they were wicked people, were French like us, but had become friends and collaborators of the Germans. To me, as the child I was then, I thought of them as evil trolls or goblins. I may not have seen them, but I knew they were there in town, checking papers, manning roadblocks, Henri said—and always dangerous. Later I was to learn more, that they would betray their own neighbors, their own families, that they were in a way worse than the Germans themselves.

It is hard to believe, I know, Vincent, but there are a few such rotten apples in any country, any community. They had become the eyes and ears of the occupiers, and they were watching everyone, watching and listening. Maman and Papa, Nancy and Henri would talk about the Milice only in whispers, and if I asked any more about them they would never answer my questions. All they would say was that if anyone ever came onto the farm, in a wide blue beret and a brown shirt, and carrying a gun, I must keep away, and hide.

Out of town, living in our caravan on the farm with Nancy and Henri and Lorenzo, we were at least far away from all that. I felt we had come to an oasis of peace and safety and tranquillity in the marshes, which I hoped the rest of the world could not touch. We saw no German soldiers, no swastika flags, no brown-shirted Milice. There was no one watching us. We lived in our caravan, hidden away from the world, in a walled yard just across the farmyard from the house and the barn, where the remains of the carousel were safely stored, waiting to be repaired.

When it came to rebuilding the carousel, it seemed the Charbonneau family and the Sully family complemented each other perfectly. Papa had been a woodcarver all his life—he and Maman had made the carousel after all, the caravan too—and Henri was a blacksmith and a mechanic, as well as a farmer. Farmers from all around brought their horses to him for shoeing, and he had been mending machinery all his working life.

And in those early days on the farm, there was much talk of our plans for the carousel, how we were going to rebuild it, who would do what, what had to be done first, where we would get the materials from, the wood, the paint, everything. But then, somehow, after a week or two, all the talk and the planning seemed to stop. Everyone was busy with the farm, with the fishing, the cheese-making. The carousel was hardly being mentioned anymore. Even Papa, who had been so determined to rebuild it, always seemed to find something else more urgent to be getting on with out on the farm.

All of us, I noticed, were staying well clear of the barn. None of us went inside. The doors stayed closed. And I knew why. I think it was the same for all of us. We did not want to have to go in there again, and see the carousel in ruins. The memory was painful enough without being reminded of it. So the wreck of the carousel lay scattered in the dark of the barn, abandoned, but never forgotten. "

CHAPTER 16

Grette Grette

"Maman had found a real soul mate in Nancy. The two of them worked together, collecting herbs and honey, making the sheep's cheese, so that Nancy had plenty to sell on market days in town.

As for Lorenzo and me, we were left mostly to our own devices, which we loved. We were having the best of times, running in and out of each other's homes. The farm and the marshes were our playground. His friends—the farm animals, the flamingos and egrets and the terrapins—were all my friends too now, but not the frogs. I did not like frogs, I told him. For Roma people, they were bad luck. I should never have told him that, because whenever he caught a frog after that he would dangle it at me and chase me with it. But then he would always put it back in the water afterward. In time, he even persuaded me to touch one, to stroke one. Bad things happened I decided, not because of frogs, but because of bad people who occupied your country, or wore brown shirts and berets, Milice people, troll people. It wasn't the fault of the frogs.

It is difficult to say how long we lived these happy times. Time means little to you when you are young—but you know that, Vincent. You do not even notice it passing. But pass it did. Sadly, the day arrived when the war came to us. It would not leave us in our peace.

Lorenzo and I had been riding out around the farm, checking the sheep on Cheval, Lorenzo riding up in front of Henri, me clinging on behind. We came clattering back into the yard to find a dozen or so German soldiers gathered outside the farmhouse. There were raised voices. Nancy, Maman, and Papa were there, confronting them, arguing with them. As we rode up, one of the soldiers had lifted his rifle, and was pointing it straight at Henri.

"What's going on here?" Henri demanded.

"They want to buy our chickens and eggs. I told them no," Nancy said. "But they don't listen." Henri lifted me down off Cheval, dismounted himself, and then helped Lorenzo down too. Lorenzo did not hesitate. Before anyone could stop him, he walked right up to the soldier who was threatening Henri, shouting at him, pushing him. He grabbed the rifle and threw it to the ground. Nancy was trying to hold on to him, to restrain him, but Lorenzo was so agitated, so angry, that Henri had to help her with him. By now, the soldier had picked up his rifle and had turned it on Lorenzo.

Then came a commanding voice from behind me, and one that I recognized. It was the giant soldier from town, the one with the white hair who limped and carried a stick. He was hurrying across the farmyard, reprimanding the soldier as he came, waving his stick at him. The rifle was lowered at once.

The giant soldier came over to us, and saluted. "We have our orders," he said. "We have been sent into the countryside to find food. We need food for the army, for our soldiers, you understand."

"I understand well enough," Nancy told him, "but you must understand also that we need our chickens for ourselves. Neither they nor their eggs are for sale. I have told your soldiers this." Nancy was calming Lorenzo as best she could, but he was still shouting, still upset.

"You have nothing we can buy, *madame*?" the soldier said. "We will, of course, pay a fair price."

Henri intervened. "You heard my wife," he said quietly. "We will not sell you anything, no matter what price you pay. You are not welcome here. You can see your soldiers have upset Lorenzo, my son. Now please go."

I remember looking up at the two men, from one to the other. Both were determined; both were proud. A flock of flamingos flying overhead broke the silence. We all looked up.

"Flam flam!" cried Lorenzo joyfully, clapping his hands, jumping up and down.

The giant soldier was looking directly at me now, then at Maman and Papa. He was nodding. "Ah yes, I remember now, the carousel family," he said. "I see. So you are two families living out here. And you two children are not brother and sister after all. I understand." He nodded slowly. None of us spoke. The silence about me was filled with sudden tension. There were fearful looks exchanged that I did not understand, but that made me suddenly fearful too.

The soldier saluted again, and turned away. "*Kommen Sie!*" he ordered his men, and they all drifted away across the farmyard. It was a small victory, and it should have felt good, but the giant soldier now knew who we were and where we were. We had been hiding away on the farm, and our enemy had discovered us.

Henri was trying to usher us all into the farmhouse when it happened. A shot rang out behind us. I looked up to see an egret above us stuttering in its flight, then falling, gliding on wings outstretched, floating down into the farm-yard, where it bounced once, and was still.

We saw the soldier who had shot it. He was bowing to his friends, accepting their applause, joining in their rau-cous cheering. Then they were running back toward the fallen egret to retrieve it. But Lorenzo was there before them, on his knees beside the bird, stroking its feathers.

I ran after him, and was trying to console him, when the soldiers arrived, breathless and elated. They would have pushed us aside had the giant soldier not been there to control them, to bring them to their senses. They were contrite almost at once and silent. No one spoke. The wind ruffled the dead egret's feathers. Lorenzo was bending over him, trying to breathe life into him. But he could see it was hopeless, and soon stopped. He looked up at us in despair, showing us the blood on his hands.

"Grette grette," he moaned, rocking back and forth.

We could not understand a word the giant soldier was shouting at his men as he formed them up to march them away, but his anger was evident. He was still reprimanding them as they marched off down the farm track.

Long after they had gone, Lorenzo stayed there, kneeling by the egret for hour after hour, stroking its feathers, wailing a lament, the same note over and over again, and rocking himself over the body of the dead bird. Nancy tried everything to persuade him to come inside, so did Henri, but he would not be moved. I knew better than to try. I stayed with him because I felt he wanted me to. The rain came later in the day, driving in over the marshes, thunder rolling and rumbling about the skies. Even then, Lorenzo knelt there, mourning the egret.

That evening, with thunder and lightning raging, Lorenzo and I buried the egret in the corner of a field, both of us soaked to the skin and shivering. Maman and Nancy came out time and again to call us in from the storm. But Lorenzo was kneeling by the grave, still grieving, and would not be moved. I could not leave him to grieve and mourn on his own.

In the end, it was Cheval neighing wildly from the field behind the barn that ended Lorenzo's vigil. Henri came running over to us.

"Renzo, you have to come!" he cried, shouting out against the storm. "Cheval is mad with fear. You know how he hates thunder. I have tried and tried to catch him, but he won't let me get near him. He has iron shoes on his feet, Renzo, and, with this lightning about, it's dangerous for him. You must come. Cheval needs you. I need you. I can't catch him. You can't do any more for the egret. Tomorrow the storm will be over, and we can all come out and put flowers on his grave, all right? But you must come now, Lorenzo. No one else can catch Cheval."

Lorenzo laid his hand on the newly turned earth, and thought for a few moments. "Grette grette," he murmured. "Grette grette." Then, his mind suddenly made up, he was up on his feet, and running toward Cheval's field, calling to him. Henri and I followed, and watched from the gate as he walked out into the field toward Cheval, who was careering around and around, crashing time and again into the fences, his neighing shrill with terror.

Lorenzo was out there now in the middle of the field, holding out his hand. "Val Val," he called softly, "Val Val. *Moi*. Renzo. *Moi*."

Almost at once the horse was calmer. Within moments, he was standing there, looking at Lorenzo, breathing heavily, tossing his head, whisking his tail. And there he stayed as Lorenzo walked slowly toward him, humming as he came. When Lorenzo stopped and waited, Cheval looked at him, and then after awhile came trotting over to him. They stood for long moments, foreheads touching. It was a miraculous sight to see. A short while later, Lorenzo was leading Cheval by his mane, out of the field and back into his stable. There he rubbed him down and fed him, before Nancy took Lorenzo firmly by the hand, and at last managed to persuade him to come back into the house.

"Sausage, Renzo," she said. "Hot bath, Renzo."

"Sausage sausage," said Lorenzo as he walked off with Nancy.

"Hot bath for you too," Maman said to me.

As we were led away from each other, Lorenzo pulled free of Nancy, and came back to me. We touched foreheads.

"Zia Zia," he said. I knew then we were friends for life. **"**

CHAPTER 17

Out of Sight, Out of Mind

"Strange to think of it now, isn't it, Vincent? *Aujourd'hui*, today, we have cars and trucks and tractors everywhere—on the roads, on the farms. But in those days it was still mostly horses, and on a farm like this just one working horse. So, when we found Cheval had gone lame the day after all that charging around in the storm, everyone knew life was not going to be easy. Henri thought it was a torn tendon that could take weeks, even months, to heal, if it ever did. Without Cheval, Henri said, all of us were going to be needed more than ever on the farm.

We all watched as Lorenzo examined Cheval's leg, then, without a word, led him away into his hospital shed and shut the door behind him. I wanted to go in with him, but Nancy caught my hand.

"He likes to be alone with them, remember?" she said. "He'll make him right again, you'll see."

"Maybe our Honey could do some of his work," Maman suggested. "She's a big strong horse."

It sounded like a good idea, but we all soon discovered that Honey had no intention whatsoever of becoming a farm horse. She would pull a caravan all day in blistering heat or driving rain. She would endure all the flies and the rutty tracks, but she would not be used to pull a dung cart out into the field. She would not be used to round up the bulls and the horses and the sheep. It was beneath her dignity. Papa and Maman and I knew well enough that she was difficult and grumpy, but we never imagined just how obstinate she could be. She would let Henri mount up, but then she would not move, no matter how much Papa shouted at her or slapped her backside. Not even the sight of a raised stick would get her going. We could all see it was no use. We would just have to work the farm ourselves without a horse, until Cheval was fit again.

I hardly saw Lorenzo over the next few days. Mostly he was inside his hospital shed, with the door closed. He came out rarely, and then only to gather flowers to put on the egret's grave. I would see him kneeling there for a few minutes, and then he would disappear back into his shed. He spoke to no one. I don't think he even knew we were there. Grieving or healing, Lorenzo wanted to be left alone.

My lessons with Nancy were soon abandoned. All of us were needed out on the farm now, Maman told me. With no horse to help, everything had to be done by hand, on foot, so it all took much longer. We were fetching and carrying to every corner of the farm, endlessly pushing wheelbarrows—that's what I remember most. I had never been so tired in all my born days. But I was happy enough to do it.

For awhile, it felt good to be busy, working alongside everyone, not to be thinking of the ruins of the carousel lying spread out in the barn. Still no one mentioned the carousel, but it was on my mind every time I passed by the barn, pushing another wheelbarrow. I could not bring myself to go in there again, and I never saw anyone else go in either.

It was the first thing I thought about every morning, and the last thing at night. That old saying—we have it in French also—"out of sight, out of mind" did not work.

As the days passed, I found I was missing Lorenzo more and more. I had not spoken to him for days on end, and was feeling miserable and lonely, and sorry for myself, I suppose. I was a child with no brothers or sisters, so I had been used to being alone, happy enough with my own company, but not anymore.

I remember I had been sent out to gather herbs and berries on my own. The mosquitoes would not leave me alone, whining about my head, biting my face, my hands. Very soon I had had enough of herbs and mosquitoes, enough of being on my own. I decided I would go looking for Lorenzo. I went to the hospital shed where I knew he must be, and called for him softly from outside the door.

"Renzo, can I come in?" I whispered. "Renzo? Renzo?" There was no reply.

I opened the door and went in. The little black calf we had been looking after was still there, lying down in the corner, beside the two orphan lambs we had been feeding.

They bleated loudly at me, and ran over to the door, butting at my legs to be fed. But there was no sign anywhere of Cheval, or of Lorenzo. Outside in the farmyard I called for him again and again. I was about to run into the house to raise the alarm, to tell Nancy, or whoever I could find, that Lorenzo was missing when I saw some horse droppings on the cobbles, and then more of them farther on down the farm track. I knew then that he had gone to Camelot. I ran as fast as I could go, brushed my way through the rushes, onto the bridge, under the gateway, and into the castle courtyard. I was right. There he was; there they both were.

Lorenzo was sitting on the stone in the middle of the courtyard, watching Cheval trotting around and around, freely, easily, with no sign of lameness at all. He smiled when he saw me, and then leaped up onto the stone, and clapped his hands.

"Va! Va! Rousel rousel!" he cried. It took me awhile to comprehend what he was talking about. Then he was singing—more shouting than singing, it was. I recognized it at once, from the rhythm rather than the tune. It was his favorite music from Maman's barrel organ, "Sur le Pont d'Avignon." Now I understood! Look, idiot, he was trying to tell me, listen! Cheval is just like Horse on the carousel, going around and around, with the music playing.

He was beckoning me to join him on the stone. So I climbed up to be beside him. We stood there, looking out over the marshes and the pink lakes, toward the blue of the sea beyond, both of us bellowing out "Sur le Pont d'Avignon." Suddenly he stopped singing.

"Flam flam!" he breathed. "Flam flam!" It took me awhile to see them standing there in the shallows, because they were so still. "Hundred twenty-two," Lorenzo said. "Hundred twenty-two." I turned to see him standing there stiffly, balanced on one leg, his neck extended forward, his head turning. He honked softly, smiling as he did so. "Zia Zia," he said lovingly. "Guin Guin." We touched foreheads.

Walking back with him that day up the track to the farm, each of us taking turns to lead Cheval, the world seemed mended and whole again, despite the Germans in the town, despite the destruction of our carousel. All was right again, our troubles and fears set aside, forgotten.

That evening we all celebrated together over a meal in

the caravan. It was Maman's favorite dish, and mine too, an omelette of ham and tomatoes and onions and zucchini, and for Lorenzo all the sausage he could eat. He was even offering it around he was so happy. We were all so relieved to have him back with us, and to have Cheval well again. **"**

CHAPTER 18

Missing, Gone!

"If Lorenzo brought us joy and laughter, he also brought us worries. I had understood well enough by this time that, for Nancy and Henri, Lorenzo's habit of wandering off could be serious, that we all had to be aware of where he was and what he was doing. We might have five pairs of eyes between us now, but this was still never easy, not on the farm.

There were times, almost every day, when someone would say: "Where's Lorenzo? Anyone seen Lorenzo?" There was no panic: looking for Lorenzo was routine. We'd go off, calling for him around the farmyard, down to Camelot, or out onto the marshes.

Sooner or later, one of us always found him, usually me

because I knew best where he might be. If he heard us calling, he would always answer, "Renzo Renzo!" He would never hide from us. He just liked wandering off.

But, lately, Nancy told me she had noticed a change in Lorenzo. He was more tired than usual, preoccupied, just not himself. She would find him curled up asleep during the daytime, and that was unusual for Lorenzo. She asked me to keep a special eye on him, so I said I would. I didn't really understand why she was so worried. Lorenzo seemed happy enough when I was with him. He didn't seem any different to me. So I forgot all about what Nancy had said. I just put it out of my mind, I suppose.

One morning, after a night battling mosquitoes, we were woken early in our caravan by the sound of footsteps running across the yard. My first thoughts were that the German soldiers had come back. But then I recognized Henri's voice, frantic with worry, and Nancy's too. I knew at once that it must be about Lorenzo. Papa opened the door.

Nancy was calling out to him: "He's missing, gone! He hasn't slept in his bed. He's been gone all night! He's never gone off at nighttime before. Never."

We were out there searching for hours. He was not

sitting on the upturned rowing boat by the lake. I ran down to Camelot and called for him there. There was no reply. I rode out with Henri on Cheval all around the farm, splashed through the shallow pink lakes out to the islands where the flamingos gathered and nested. They took off in their hundreds at our approach, honking at us in indignation. We had disturbed their peace. We rode around all the lakes, searched every field, went in amongst the herds of horses and bulls, fearful he might have been trampled, then set off down the farm track, along the canal, toward town. Hiding away as I had been on the farm, it was a long time since I had been there. But we had forgotten all about that. We had to find Lorenzo. Nothing else mattered.

Once there, Henri asked everyone we met whether they had seen Lorenzo. German soldiers were forming up outside the *mairie*. The giant soldier was with them, inspecting them. He stood a head higher than any of them—you could not miss him. He looked up and saw us. He lifted his hand in recognition. Henri asked in the cafés, outside the shops. No one had seen Lorenzo.

By the time we rode back up the farm track along the

canal, I could tell Henri was fearing the worst. He didn't say anything, but he was walking Cheval ever more slowly, and deliberately so, stopping often to search the banks now, and the canal itself. He was not calling for Lorenzo anymore. Now I was fearing the worst too.

As we came into the yard in front of the house, we saw Nancy and Maman outside. They were clinging on to each other and sobbing.

"You found him?" Henri cried out. "You found him? Tell me, tell me."

They could speak no words through their tears. All Maman could do was wave us toward the barn. The doors were wide open. Henri dismounted and ran inside. I followed him.

Coming out of bright daylight into sudden darkness, I could see very little at first, but on the ground in the center of the barn there was an oil lamp glowing, flickering. I was beginning to make out the remains of the carousel spread out on the floor. They were as I remembered them, but then I looked again. Something had changed. I could see they were not as we had left them, not scattered randomly anymore.

Lorenzo was nowhere to be seen, but Papa was there, crouching down. He turned to us, his finger to his lips. I looked where he was looking. The most extraordinary sight met my eyes. Lorenzo was lying there on the ground, knees drawn up, thumb in his mouth, fast asleep, and all around him, in a great circle, lay the remains of the carousel, no longer strewn about and scattered everywhere, but gathered, the pieces fitted together: Horse together, Bull together, Elephant together, Dragon together. And the rides were all in the right order too. Every one of them was where it should be. The winding gear lay in the middle, twisted, but pieced together, the cranking handle beside it. Maman's barrel organ was there, the generator too—all broken, but recognizable. It was all recognizable, even the coronet of flying flamingos that had once crowned the carousel.

Maman and Nancy were there with us by now, smiling through their tears.

"We never thought to look in here," Nancy said, keeping her voice low, "not till we had looked everywhere else. I suppose we didn't want to come in. We searched all over, called for him everywhere. He was in here all the time, fast asleep. He must have spent night after night doing this, putting it together again, his 'rousel.' He can hardly put two words together, but he can do this."

"You know what he's trying to tell us, don't you?" Maman said.

Papa was nodding. "I think I understand the message," he replied. "He wants us to get on with it, make it what it once was."

"We have to bring it back to its glory," Maman told him. "No more hiding it away, no more putting it off. We know what we have got to do."

Papa was walking around the carousel, hands on hips, looking down at it. "We won't be able to recover all of it. There's lots we'll just have to burn, whether we like it or not. Looking at it now, I'd say we could save maybe half of the rides; the rest I can carve again. And you can paint them all, Maman, can't you?"

"I can try to fix the machinery, all the ironwork," said Henri. "It'll take time, though."

That was the moment Lorenzo stirred, woke, and saw us all standing there.

"Rousel rousel!" he said, smiling up at us. Then he was on his feet at once, whirling around and around, showing us all the animals one by one. "Val! Bull! Agon! Lephant!" Then he was leaping over everything, and running around the outside, around the frieze of flying pink flamingos. "Flam flam! Flam flam!" he cried, clapping his hands with joy.

Suddenly he stopped in his tracks, as still as a statue, and silent. He was looking past us toward the doorway. We turned. Standing there was the giant soldier, his rifle over his shoulder. For some time, no one spoke. Fear crept up my back and into my neck, into the roots of my hair. I moved closer to Maman, felt her arm come around my shoulder, and felt her fear too.

"*Entschuldigung*—I am sorry," the soldier began, with a bow of his head and a salute. "I see you have found your boy. Lorenzo, I think you call him. That is good. We heard in town that you were looking for him, so I came to see if I could help to search. I have soldiers with me outside. I am pleased you have found him. You must be very happy." He was looking down at the carousel spread out on the ground.

"*Wunderbar!*" he exclaimed. "*Wunderbar.* Wonderful.

One day this carousel will turn again, and the music will play. One day. Nothing is more important than our children. In this uniform, I am Caporal Willi Brenner. Under this uniform, I am Herr Willi Brenner, husband, father, *und Lehrer*—teacher—from Tübingen. I wish to say this, that your carousel is very important. And do you know why? It is because it makes children happy. I think this is the most important thing we can do—make our children happy. You still have much work to do, but, when it is done, it will be good work, because it will make your children happy; it will make many children happy. If ever there is any help I can give you—"

"We shall manage," said Papa, his voice so cold I was ashamed of him.

"I am sure you will," the Caporal replied. "*Guten Tag, meine Freunde*—good day." He was hesitating. He seemed to have something else on his mind, but was unsure whether to say it or not.

He lowered his voice. "I want you to remember what I say now." He was looking directly at Maman and Papa as he spoke. "It is important, very important. I know that you are Roma people. Here in the marshes you are out of sight, and that is good. But, sooner or later, people will get to know. My soldiers, they go into town sometimes, and soldiers talk. The Milice, the Gestapo, they have eyes and ears everywhere. If they come, I may be able to warn you, but I cannot stop them. You understand? You must be ready always to go, to have somewhere to hide."

Then Papa said: "But if they have eyes and ears everywhere then they will come anyway. So what's the point in running? And where would we run to? We will not run. Our family has lived in and around these marshes for thousands of years. It is our home, and we will stay. Besides, we have the carousel to finish."

"Yes," said the Caporal. "All that you say is true. And yes, you have the carousel to finish. That is most important." With that, he turned and limped out of the barn.

Maman came up and put her hand on Papa's shoulder. "They can't all be bad," she said. "There are good ones amongst them."

"They all wear the uniform," Papa replied. "Never forget that."

CHAPTER 19

Killing Dragons

"I do remember that from that day onward, busy though we still were out on the farm, nothing mattered more than the rebuilding of our carousel. There were long and purposeful discussions in the barn, during which the most difficult decisions were made, all of us standing over the remains, crouching over them, walking around them. We were having to make up our minds about which precious fragment was worth keeping, which was too damaged and beyond repair, which was still intact enough, and strong enough, to become part of our new carousel.

Of one thing we were now quite sure: that we would never give up as we had so nearly done before. We were determined that the Charbonneau Carousel would one day be turning again in the town square, the children laughing, the music playing. Lorenzo had given us all such heart and hope. He had shown us there was a way forward, that there had to be. We just had to overcome whatever difficulties and problems lay ahead, and get on with it. One way or another, we would do it. And, though no one said it at the time, I have always thought that those few words of encouragement spoken by the giant soldier—the Caporal as we came to call him—in the barn that day helped spur us on as well.

Every piece that was to be discarded had to have Lorenzo's approval. He would stand by the barn doors, making quite sure nothing was being carried out that could or should be saved. He was particularly adamant that no fragment, however small or insignificant, from the frieze of flying pink flamingos was ever to be taken away. He understood, as we all did, that the animal rides, the poles the children held on to—which served as roof supports too— the flooring, the roof, all these had to be strong; and that most of the carousel was so damaged it would have to be completely replaced. Many times I saw Lorenzo reaching out to touch some fragment of one of the animal rides as it was carried past him, as if saying good-bye to it for the last time.

You may have noticed on your travels, Vincent, that out on these marshes there are very few trees. They struggle here to reach any size at all. If they grow to any height, the wind will soon blow them down. Trees do not like wind, or salt. Here we have both, and in great abundance too. Just finding enough wood for our fires and stoves to get us through the winters was always hard. *C'est toujours comme ça!* It still is! A fire is the heart of every home. Wood is precious.

Now, for this one winter ahead at least, neither family—either in the farmhouse or in our caravan—would have to worry. None of the unusable wood from the ruins of the carousel, however small, was allowed to go to waste. We sheltered our pile of scraps and splinters and shards under the caravan, and Henri and Nancy and Lorenzo stacked theirs away in the woodshed behind the farmhouse.

Nancy told me how upset Lorenzo would be if he ever saw anything from the carousel going onto the fire, or into the stove so she always had to wait until he was out of the house before burning anything. We felt much the same in the caravan, especially Papa, who of course knew every piece of it so intimately. But on the coldest of nights that winter— if I am honest—Papa and Maman and I, we were quite happy to be warm.

It was during those winter months that we began to try to gather in the rest of the timber we knew we were going to need to rebuild the carousel. With no trees to cut down on the farm, and no spare money to buy any wood, we had to make the long trek by horse and cart down to the sea to scour the beaches and dunes for any washed-up timber. Winter storms often brought in quite a harvest of wood from the sea. We made several trips, some more successful than others. Papa and Maman had an idea where it might be best to concentrate our searches. We had often traveled the shores of the Camargue coast, even scoured the beaches for firewood, especially around Saintes-Maries-de-la-Mer, a Roma town we had been to often. Maman and Papa knew the winds and tides there, all the beaches where any flotsam was most likely to be washed ashore.

One lucky day, out on one of those windswept beaches, after a cold and fruitless morning of tramping the sand and finding nothing but dead and dried-up jellyfish, we came across a veritable treasure trove of wooden planks, some of them half buried. In fact, I was the one who spotted them first—and I've always been very proud of that. I remember Lorenzo counting them at once—twenty-seven it was—and then he did a flamingo dance on the beach in celebration. Soon we were joining in, all of us honking with him in triumph.

Breathless with dancing, we laid all the planks out on the sand, and then stood back, admiring our find. Papa examined them, and said they were pine, just as the original floor of the carousel had been, that they could not have been in the water for long, and would be perfect. It may not be all we needed, by any means, he told us, but it was a start, and a great one. We did have a few damaged floor planks that we had saved from the remains of the carousel, which could be used again, but we would still need to find much more timber from somewhere, so we had to keep looking.

It was a good thing we did too. Farther along the beach

that same day, we came across a couple of washed-up tree trunks, whitened by sun and wind, that Papa said might just provide enough wood from which he could carve at least two of the rides. It was a wonderful day that cheered Papa and all of us to no end. We loaded all the wood onto our cart. On the way home, we sang and sang, mostly "Sur le Pont d'Avignon," because that's what Lorenzo wanted to hear, of course. Our hearts were full of happiness and hope.

Most of the work, as we began to restore the carousel, was done during the evenings, Papa in the barn, busy at his carving, Henri at his forge, hammering away at the ironwork, at the circular frames for the floor and roof of the carousel, beating them back into shape. Lorenzo and I would be there with him, Lorenzo working the bellows, keeping the fire hot. I was used as the water carrier, fetching and carrying from the lakeside all the buckets of water Henri needed for cooling the iron.

I hurried back with every bucket, because I loved to be there when he plunged the red-hot iron into the water, filling our faces with billowing steam. *J'ai adoré ça!* I loved that!

Progress was slow, but bit by bit, as the weeks passed, we could begin to see that all we had to do was keep working at it, that one day Maman's barrel organ would play again, and Papa's carousel would turn again, and one day the pink flamingos on the frieze would fly again.

I think it was because I was beginning to feel trapped on the farm that I kept asking Maman and Papa if I could go into town with Nancy and Henri on market days, taking Lorenzo with us, and be there with them, selling on the stall, but both Papa and Maman forbade it. They would not say why. I could tell there was something they were hiding from me. Papa in particular wouldn't hear of it. When I argued, and asked him why yet again, he just said I was to do as I was told for a change. We ended up shouting at each other, with him grabbing me by the shoulders and shaking me, with me yelling out the worst insults I knew at him, then running off into the marshes.

Maman came after me, and caught up with me. She was in tears too. I kept on and on at her to tell me why I shouldn't go.

"I know about the German soldiers," I cried. "I know

about the Milice. You told me! But we haven't done anything wrong, have we? Why can't I go, why?"

In the end, to stop me crying, I think, to calm me down, she told me. And only then did I understand why they had not wanted to tell me.

"The Germans, they don't like Roma people, Kezia. I mean, more than most people they don't like us," she said. "So it is best to keep out of their way, as Papa told you. And the Milice, the brown shirts—some of them are worse than the Germans. They hate Roma people, all of us. They hate Jewish people too. You remember Madame Salomon at your school? Well, first she lost her job only because she was Jewish. They did not want her teaching their children. Then, and this happened only a couple of weeks ago, Henri told us, they came for her, the Milice it was, and took her away, her and her husband. No one has seen them since. And I don't think anyone will. Jewish people, Roma people—the Germans, the Milice, they want to be rid of us. That is why you cannot go into town with Nancy, Henri, and Lorenzo. Now do you understand? We didn't want to tell you all this. We didn't want to frighten you, to upset you. So you mustn't blame Papa. He doesn't want you anywhere near them, and neither do I. And they hate children like Lorenzo too."

"Why?" I asked her. "How could anyone hate Lorenzo?"

She sighed deeply, sadly. "Because he is different, Kezia—the same reason they hate us, and the Jews, because we are different. There is no other reason."

After that, I remember I prayed to Saint Sarah every night to look after Madame Salomon. I would think of her whenever I looked at the icon of Saint Sarah in the corner of the caravan. Papa and I forgave each other for all the harsh words, but it took awhile. Neither of us forgave easily.

The farm was our home now, our haven from the world, and, after everything Maman had told me, I was happy to stay there. But we had to work, both Lorenzo and I. Feeding the hens and horses was our main task, which we loved to do. But mucking out, spreading manure, picking stones off the fields, weeding, and endlessly filling up buckets of water for the animals, none of this was much fun. Lorenzo knew how and when it was best to skip off unnoticed, and so we often ended up sitting watching flamingos from the upturned boat, or nursing his animals in his hospital shed.

It was a strange thing to see, but he would talk more fluently to a young flamingo, or a sick calf, than he ever did to people. When he was with them, the words, even sentences, seemed to flow out of him. They didn't all make sense, not to me, but they did to them. No, I mean it, Vincent—and I know it sounds ridiculous—but I am telling you that all his creatures would really listen, really understand.

And then we would run off down the farm track to Camelot, where we would hide away, and play for hours on end. Sometimes, sitting on the rock in the courtyard, I would read him stories from his King Arthur book again, which always kept him happy, and it kept Nancy happy too. I must have been practicing a lot, Nancy said, because my reading was making great progress. But the truth was that I only practiced with this one book, so I knew it almost by heart by now, as Lorenzo did. He would act out his favorite stories as I read them, often echoing every word of the story as I was reading it.

I loved being his "Guin"—I noticed he only called me that in his castle. It was the only place he ever bowed down to me too, the only place he pulled a sword from the stone, or acted out his sword fights or killed dragons. There were no dragons in the stories. He made them up. I think he loved killing dragons because he loved saving me.

"Agon agon!" he would cry triumphantly, thrusting his sword down another fiery dragon's throat, and saving me yet again from a horrible death.

One afternoon, we had abandoned our farmwork as usual and we were playing in Camelot. I was sitting on the stone, and Lorenzo was swishing his stick, slaying more dragons. We both heard it at the same moment, a distant rumbling, not of a storm, not of thunder, as I first thought, but of engines. I stopped reading. Lorenzo stopped killing dragons. A car was coming down the farm track. It sounded now more like several cars. Standing up on our stone, we could see over the walls and the rushes beyond. There was a car, but behind it came trucks, three trucks, four trucks, a whole convoy of them, and they were stopping on the farm track just by the bridge, German army trucks, with white crosses on the sides. There were barked orders, and then soldiers were jumping down out of the trucks, and running across the bridge, their boots thundering. They came pouring through the gateway, filling the courtyard, surrounding us, rifles at the ready.

We stood on our story stone, stunned and fearful. I felt Lorenzo's hand creep into mine. He squeezed it tight, and I squeezed back, each of us filling the other with the courage we needed.

"Agon agon," he whispered to me. He still had the stick in his hand, his dragon-killing spear, and, for a moment, I feared he might jump down and run at one of them and spear him in the throat. I held his hand tighter, pulled him closer. "

CHAPTER 20

Agon Agon!

"That was when I saw the Caporal come limping into the courtyard, his stick in one hand, a map in the other.

"Agon agon!" Lorenzo was shouting down at him from our high stone, slapping his chest again and again. I never saw him so furious, not even in the town square in Aigues-Mortes that day when the Germans arrived. I could hear the tears in his voice, tears of rage and defiance. "Lot Lot! *Roi, moi, roi, moi!*"

The Caporal recognized him at once, and did not seem at all offended by his anger. "Hello, Lorenzo," he said, waving the map at him. "It is me, Caporal Brenner. It is good to see you again. You remember me? Caporal Willi Brenner. We have met before, no? This must be the place I was looking for on my map."

"Capo!" Lorenzo shouted, shaking his fist. "Capo Capo! Agon agon!"

"What are you doing here?" came a voice, Henri's voice, from behind us. He was standing there with Papa at his side. "This is private property. You have no right. This is our place, our farm. This is Lorenzo's castle."

The Caporal folded his map, and saluted Henri. He produced from his pocket a piece of paper. "I am afraid I do have the right, *monsieur*," he went on, as he handed it over. "I have my orders. You will see here on this paper that the German Army is taking over this fortification. We will be building it up, strengthening the walls, making it strong again. We will be bringing guns here, big guns for our sea defenses, against the Americans, should they be foolish enough to land here. We will do our best not to inconvenience you, *monsieur*. But from now on this place, for the time being, is to be considered the property of the German Army. My men will be putting up a barbed-wire fence today.

I shall be the Caporal in charge of the building works. No one else will be allowed to come in here, and this includes children, of course. It will not be safe for them. We shall be camping here tonight. All the building works for the bunker and gun emplacements, and the garrison we will need for the soldiers, all will start tomorrow. This will be our home from now on. And you and your children, you have to leave now. I am sorry."

The long silence that followed was a standoff. The Caporal and his soldiers were not going to move, and neither were we. I had the impression that Lorenzo had understood every word that had been spoken, for his hand gripped mine tighter and tighter, and I knew it was not in fear but in determination, defiance.

In the end, it was Henri who broke the silence. He spoke very quietly and deliberately. "The Romans built this place a long time ago, Caporal, for the same reason as you, to make defenses, to make a fort. Our ancestors were here when they came. Like you, they were occupiers. They came and they went. They were driven out, as you will be. We stay in the Camargue, just as the flamingos stay. We have always stayed. It is our place. Our time will come again, and you and your men will be gone. Meanwhile, we shall keep away, just so long as you and your men also stay away from the farm. You make your war here if you must, Caporal. We want only to be left in peace with our children on our farm. Let that be the agreement between us."

"It is agreed," the Caporal replied.

Papa was calling us down from the stone. The Caporal came and offered his hand to help us down. Lorenzo and I stood there, towering above him. Lorenzo was ignoring his proffered hand. Instead, he was pointing his stick at him, right at his throat.

Speaking very quietly, he said, "Agon agon." I knew what he meant, as did Papa and Henri, but the Caporal and all the soldiers simply looked bewildered.

Then, still holding hands, we both jumped down, and walked away with Papa and Henri, leaving Camelot behind us. Lorenzo strode on ahead over the bridge and up the track, past the convoy of lorries, shoulders hunched, head bent, kicking out at the stones in his fury. He stopped suddenly, and let out a great cry of anger that became a wailing, then a roar of anguish that echoed over the marshes, sending the flamingos flying. Seeing them overhead calmed his rage, but brought on tears. I ran to him and we stood there on the farm track, forehead to forehead, hands on each other's shoulders, the flamingos honking above us, as if they knew, as if they were singing to soothe his sadness, all our sadnesses.

If we had not had the work on the carousel to do, to occupy our hearts and hands and minds, I think we might have been overwhelmed by this new invasion. Lorenzo felt it badly. There were times when he could not put it out of his mind. They had captured his castle, driven him out. Day after day, he grieved for his Camelot, finding consolation only in the privacy of his animal hospital, where he could be heard humming and singing to them.

He did go missing from the animal hospital in the days that followed, but I always knew where I could find him. He would be down the farm track, standing by the barbed-wire perimeter the soldiers had put up. There was no way through now. The bridge, the whole castle, his beloved Camelot, had been wired off. There were sentries guarding the wire and the bridge, patrolling the walls.

If ever we came too close, they would shout at us to go away, and some of them would laugh at Lorenzo, mocking him, how he talked, how he walked, calling him all sorts of names I did not understand, except one because they shouted it in French: "*Garçon fou!* Crazy boy! Hey there, you crazy boy!" I knew that Lorenzo understood, that it hurt him, but he stayed. He would not be driven away.

I would stand with him and watch, as the lorries came and went, day in, day out, bringing in more and more building supplies, the soldiers fetching and carrying everything over the bridge into the castle. We were there, watching together, when the diggers arrived and began work inside and around the walls. Day after day, they were there, working almost constantly. Constant too was the sound of hammering and sawing.

Sometimes we saw parties of workers come shuffling by under guard, bedraggled and thin, barefoot some of them. When I first saw them, I did not know who they were, nor where they were from. They were not local people. I recognized none of them. They scarcely looked at us as they passed by. It was as if we were not there, as if we and they lived in different worlds.

Every day more concrete was being brought in and the scaffolding and the walls were going up ever higher. Before our eyes they were transforming the place into a huge concrete bunker. I hated to stand there, watching the desecration of Lorenzo's Camelot, but once there I could not leave him on his own, not with the soldiers so close. It was never easy to persuade him to come home. The only way was to tempt him, to tell him that Cheval was missing him, or maybe that there were hundreds of flamingos waiting for him on the lake, turning their heads this way and that, looking for him. Any mention of the carousel might help to tempt him away too. Papa was busy carving the head of Bull, or the trunk of Elephant, I would tell him. Or I would remind him that Henri was mending the workings of the barrel organ, that he'd almost finished the repairs on the generator. I told him anything that I thought would take his mind off the occupation and ruination of his castle, anything that would cheer his spirit. Sooner or later, I would feel he was listening, that he was almost ready to come with me. Then

I would take his hand gently, and he would turn away at last and leave.

I was there doing just that one day, trying to talk him into coming home, when we saw the giant soldier, the Caporal, coming across the bridge. I had not seen him in awhile. He was carrying a long plank of wood under his arm. He raised his hand in greeting as he came down the farm track toward us.

"I have been told you have been looking for wood, for the carousel. Is this so?" Nervous of speaking to him, neither of us replied. "I hope you are rebuilding the carousel so it will be just as it was before. It was very beautiful. And I liked the music too, very much. Here." He was holding out the plank of wood, offering it to us. "We do not need this for our building work. We have enough. It will not be missed." He looked over his shoulder. "Quick, quick. I do not wish to be seen. You can carry it between you, I think. It might be useful."

I took it from him. Lorenzo stood there, stone-faced, and would not help. He did not seem to want to touch the plank. I took it because I knew we needed it, and because I felt that this was a kind and thoughtful thing the Caporal had done. My thank-you was muted, but he heard it.

He smiled and said, "*Bitte schön*—you're welcome." Then he saluted us and walked away.

When we got back to the farmhouse, they were all delighted with our "find." I told them we had found the plank floating in the canal in amongst the rushes. Lorenzo was frowning as I told my tale. He was trying to work it out, to understand why I was not telling the truth, and becoming quite agitated. It may have taken a few moments, but I think he soon realized that if I had told them the plank was a gift from the giant Caporal, from the Germans, that Henri or Papa would have insisted on taking it back, or burning it.

That evening, we were all there in the barn, looking on, as Papa sawed the Caporal's plank to just the right length, cut and planed the ends so they fitted the restored circular iron frame perfectly, then laid it down alongside the other planks from the beach. Our carousel had nearly half a floor now.

I was in bed that night when Maman came and sat beside

me. Papa was still at work on the carousel in the barn, so we were alone in the caravan.

"Kezia," she whispered, as she bent over to kiss me good night, "the wood you say you found in the canal, it was not wet."

I cried then and told her the truth. "Don't tell Papa, please," I begged her.

"I never lie to your *papa*," she said. "But not telling is not lying, not quite. I shall say nothing. But never again, Kezia, you hear me? Never again. These people are enemies. Think what they did to Madame Salomon and her family. We must not forget this."

She stayed and talked for awhile, and that was when I asked her about the strange work parties we had seen being marched into the castle day after day, why they were so badly clothed and thin, and why they spoke another language.

"They are slaves, Kezia," she told me. "Prisoners. Russians maybe, or Poles. They use them for slave labor. This, and Madame Salomon, is why I tell you it is wrong to take gifts from the Nazi occupiers. They may not all be wicked, but they do wicked things, cruel things. So never again, Kezia, you hear me? No matter how kind they seem, how much they smile."

"So Lorenzo is right," I said. "They are dragons—agons, he calls them."

"Lorenzo is right about most things," Maman told me, giving me another kiss. "You should remember that, Kezia."

CHAPTER 21

Patience Is a Virtue

Infuriatingly, frustratingly, it was at this moment in the story that Ami decided to rise up from the fireside, shake himself, scratch his ear, and then make his way across the room to the front door, where he stood, hanging his head, nose touching the door, looking miserable and needy, at which he was an expert. I had seen this performance often enough by now to know what he was asking for, and that the story was going to have to wait.

Kezia got up and pulled on her coat. "That dog is a tyrant to me." She sighed. "He will not take no for an answer. He does not like the dark on his own. He is frightened of the foxes out there, and the badgers, and the wild boar, I think. I will have to go with him."

She stopped and turned to me as she reached the door. "I was thinking again as I was telling you the story that it is so strange you being here, coming here as you have—out of the blue, I think you say. He came out of the blue also, and he was English too. He is the only other person I have ever told the story to. But he was always more interested in the flamingos. Like Lorenzo, *il adorait les flamands roses.* Flamingos were his passion."

"Who was he? Who do you mean?" I asked her.

She smiled. "He is an important part of the story," she said, "a very important part. But he comes at the end, so you will have to wait. I do not want to put the end before its time comes, the cart before the horse—I love your English expressions. I will tell you about him later. Now, as you can see, Ami needs to go outside—to do his business, I think you say. You see? Another of your delightful English expressions." Chuckling, she was gone then with Ami out into the night.

After awhile, I got up to have another look at all the photographs on the walls. There were more flamingos than people, but it was the people who really interested me. I knew who many of the faces were by now. Lorenzo loved to show them to me again and again, often touching them

tenderly, stroking them with his fingertips, then reminding me of their names too: Henri, Nancy, Renzo, Kezia.
There was one in particular, of himself, he always liked to
show me—and I could never look at it without smiling.
He must have been my age when the photograph was
taken—about eighteen or so, I guessed. He was walking
somewhere out on the marshes, being followed in stately
procession by a dozen flamingos. It wasn't comical so
much as balletic, beautiful, touching. It said everything
about Lorenzo, about his love for flamingos, and their love
for him.

From these photographs, I knew what so many of the
people in Kezia's story had looked like. Nancy was usually
smiling, and often holding hands with the two children, with
Lorenzo and Kezia, Lorenzo towering above Kezia even as
a child. There was only one photo of Henri, riding up on
Cheval in his broad-rimmed hat, a long pole in his hand.
He was staring sternly back at the camera, a herd of white
horses in the background. I had never thought of him with
a mustache, and it was a magnificent one too, until I saw
him in that photo.

There was one of the caravan, with little Kezia and her *maman* and *papa* standing proudly outside, and Honey, their bad-tempered piebald horse, grazing behind them. And beyond the caravan I could make out a walled town—Aigues-Mortes, I presumed—where so much of Kezia's story had happened.

There was only one rather faded photograph of the carousel, with Lorenzo as a boy, sitting on Horse, Kezia beside him, holding his elbow, steadying him, both having the happiest of times. And there was Papa, turning his cranking handle, and Maman beside her barrel organ. It may have been a still, silent photo in black-and-white, but it was not difficult to imagine the color, the sound, the music, the sheer fun and joy of it. And I could see the great plane tree in full leaf towering over it, in the town square.

There were a few photos too of white horses and black bulls and sheep out on the marshes, and then there were all those thirty or forty photos of flamingos. In some, the flamingos were in flight; in others, wading in their hundreds through the shallows, or taking off, or landing, or they were dancing, sitting on eggs, sleeping. Maybe my favorite one was of a flamingo at rest, her head nestling in among her feathers. All these flamingo photographs were in color, as well as the one of Lorenzo as a younger man, nose to beak with a flamingo. They were not just domestic snapshots as the black-and-white photos were. Each one was more like a photographic study of flamingo life on the marshes, flamingos of all ages, in all seasons, and each one perfectly developed.

By the time Kezia came back in with Ami awhile later, I was back on my couch, ready for her to finish her story. She read my thoughts. "It is horrible out there," she said. "Your English rain has followed you here." She was shaking herself, and enjoying it hugely. "The story can wait, Vincent. I have to be in the right mood to finish it. It is not such an easy story to tell, especially toward the end."

My heart sank. Ami lay down near the fire, head on his paws, eyeing me. He was not my favorite dog at the moment.

"It is good to see you looking so much better, Vincent," Kezia said as she made her way to the stairs to go up to bed.

"When will you tell me the rest?" I asked her.

"*Bientôt*. Soon," she replied. "Soon I will tell you, I promise. But now is not the time. It is right you should know the whole story. I want you to know just how it was, how it happened. Lorenzo would want the same. He is very fond of you, Vincent. He trusts you. Trust for him is the most important thing, and loyalty. Loyalty, as you know, is simply repeated trust. And repetition, for him, is reassurance, and reassurance is everything. He would like me to trust you with our story, all of our story, but it is for another time. Sleep well." She put her head on one side and studied me. "It is extraordinary, *vraiment extraordinaire*. You are so like him, like Alan, the other Englishman. You are much younger, of course, but you have the same deep-set eyes."

"Alan who?" I asked her.

"Patience is a virtue, Vincent. Or didn't your mother tell you that? Good night. *Bonne nuit*." And that was all she would say.

She left me with my head so full of questions that I hardly slept that night. As it turned out, in the days that followed, as I recovered—and I was regaining my strength quickly now—some questions were beginning to answer themselves anyway, in part at least.

The very next day was fine and bright, and Lorenzo wanted yet again to take me out. This time Kezia said that she thought I was well enough, but I had to take it easy and come back soon. So, at long last, I got to know for myself where I had been all this time.

I had seen so much of it, of course, in my mind, as Kezia told her story, and from the photos too: the farmhouse, the barn, the black bulls, the white horses, the marshes, the pink lakes, the flamingos. I had stood there, looking out of the windows, so I had some idea of what to expect. But now I was outside in the fresh air, in the wind, and seeing it all properly for the first time. Lorenzo was taking me by the hand, and leading me on a guided tour, talking all the while, Ami sometimes following us, sometimes not. Ami did what he pleased.

Most of Lorenzo's talk was about "flam flam," so I knew the tour was likely to be mainly a flamingo tour, and so it proved. And, wherever he led me, the story Kezia had been telling me took on a landscape, a new life, new meaning, and sometimes also a new perplexity.

When Lorenzo showed me into the barn, for instance, there was no sign of a carousel anywhere. Where had it gone? And when he took me, as I hoped he would, down the farm track along the canal, and walked me over the bridge to see the castle, his Camelot, it was not at all as I had imagined. Yes, there were the bare, ruined walls of an old castle, and a grassy courtyard with a great stone in the middle. But what of the concrete bunker and the gun emplacement that Kezia had told me the giant Caporal and his German soldiers had built there? There was no sign of any of it.

I so wanted to ask Lorenzo about it all, but I knew that I mustn't, that Kezia would not have wanted me to, that it might be too intrusive, too upsetting for him. She had always been so careful never to tell me the story in his hearing. And anyway I would have probably been unable to understand most of what he might try to tell me. So I said nothing, asked nothing. Kezia would soon explain everything, I thought, I hoped.

That walk down the farm track to Camelot, with Lorenzo holding my hand all the way, delighting in showing me his kingdom, was the first of many walks. Every time I went out with him, my step felt stronger, my breathing came more easily. I was tiring less quickly, going farther and farther afield every day. Once he took me back to the very place he had found me, on the long, straight road across the marshes. He explained all this by dramatizing it, lying down and being me. Then he was picking me up and carrying me a few steps, Ami cavorting around us, as if he remembered too. Maybe he did.

Afterward, we walked to the lakeside and we sat together silently on his upturned rowing boat, watching a flock of flamingos out on the lake. We saw them in their hundreds, stepping out through the pink shallows, making their take-off runs on the water, then lifting into the sky, higher, higher, accompanied by a chorus of celebratory honking. They came back a few minutes later to land close to us, their feet seeming to tread the water, tiptoeing over it with hardly a splash as they touched down.

"Two hundred fifteen," Lorenzo cried, clapping his hands. "Flam flam! Flam flam!" He held up his fingers to show me, two fingers, then one, and then five. I knew he was not guessing.

On the way back to the farmhouse, he showed me into his hospital shed, as I had been hoping he would. He had three flamingo fledglings in there now. He fed them, and let me feed them too. As he crouched down and breathed on them, they nibbled his lips. One was weaker than the others and I could see he was worried about it. He sat beside this one, held it on his lap, breathing over it, rocking back and forth, humming a quiet tune.

It was the evening of that same day, the day I had seen the two hundred and fifteen flamingos with Lorenzo, that Kezia and I found ourselves alone together again by the fireside. I had been longing to ask her about the whereabouts of the carousel, to find out about the gun emplacement she had told me the Germans had built on the ruins of Lorenzo's Camelot, and that was certainly not there now. But how could I ask her without implying that I thought she had been making this whole story up? I couldn't ask her; I couldn't do it. I just had to wait for her to tell me as and when the moment was right for her. It wasn't a long wait, but it seemed like it at the time.

CHAPTER 22

An Accident, a Casualty

Lorenzo had gone out for one of his late-evening walks into the marshes as usual, just as he had the night he found me, and Ami had gone with him.

"I hope he doesn't find another English boy out there," Kezia laughed as she sat down by the fire. "We have nowhere else for him to sleep. I think we shall be alone for awhile, Vincent, enough time maybe to finish the story. *Alors*, if I remember, I think I had just brought home the Caporal's plank of wood, is that right? And Maman had discovered I was lying about finding it in the canal. It was very silly of me to lie to Maman, because she could always read me like a book. Anyway, she kept her word and didn't tell Papa, which was a great relief to me. I hated Papa to be angry with me. He only had to look at me disapprovingly, and it was like a knife in my heart.

"Papa and Henri were of one mind about the German soldiers now garrisoned in the castle. I think it was one of the reasons they became such close friends so quickly. They were of one mind about so many things. There should be as little association with the Germans as possible, they said. We should all keep away from the place and have nothing to do with them. But Lorenzo had a mind of his own, and, regardless of what they said, and regardless of the endless taunting and mocking of the German soldiers, he would take me back there every day, down the farm track, to watch all the comings and goings.

Great concrete bunkers were growing like warts all around his Camelot. I knew that witnessing this hideous transformation broke his heart, but that all the same he had to see it for himself. His beloved Camelot was being turned into a grim gray fortress, with barbed wire and ditches all around. They had captured his castle, taken it over, created a monstrosity of it, and made it their own. He hated it, but he had to be there.

We were there the day the big guns were brought in. They came in a convoy of transporters, two enormous guns covered in canvas, the size and shape of the barrels quite obvious—they were so long there was no disguising them. We rushed home and told Maman, the first person we could find. But Papa was there too and he overheard.

"Haven't I told you and told you, Kezia?" he said, lifting my chin to make me look at him, to make me know he meant it. "Stay away. Don't go near there, you hear me?"

But I had no choice. Wherever Lorenzo went these days, he insisted I had to go with him. He never wandered off on his own anymore. But every time we went there he was becoming more and more agitated. Often I had to hold him back when he went to shout at the soldiers on the bridge, or even throw stones at them. Their taunting only made him worse, more angry and upset. He was strong when he was angry like this, and it was all I could do to restrain him. I knew I could not hold him for long. Sooner or later, he would break free of me.

I needed to distract him. I tried talking to him softly, using his language, talking his way, of "rousel," and "Val," of "flam flam." It did not always work, but any mention of "flam flam" was effective, especially if we were touching foreheads as I was saying it. The sound of that word calmed him like no other, so I would repeat it again and again, and the more he echoed it back to me, the calmer he became. Then I could walk him away, back up the track to the farm and out of harm's way.

Once away from his Camelot, he seemed to be able to put out of his mind what was going on down there, for awhile at least. He would often lead me by the hand straight to his animal hospital where he would sit down beside his rescued flamingo fledglings and rock himself back and forth, his eyes closed, humming to them. Within a few minutes, he was completely calm again. I saw then, for the first time, that Lorenzo's love for his flamingos, for all his creatures, was as beneficial to him, to his state of mind, and to his happiness, as he was to theirs. They cared for him as much as he cared for them. This really was mutual love, mutual healing.

I must have been so preoccupied with looking after Lorenzo, watching flamingos with him from the upturned boat, with all the restoration work on the carousel going on in the barn, that I scarcely gave any thought to those big guns again. I knew they were there now, of course, but I could not see them. So I forgot about them, I suppose. The German soldiers never came near us, and had tired of mocking him now, and after awhile Lorenzo wanted less and less to go down the farm track to revisit his Camelot. I think in the end he must have realized it only made him sad, and so he kept away. I was glad of that. I hated being anywhere near the place.

All this time, progress on the rebuilding of the carousel was slow. We only left the farm at all these days if we were going on trips to the coast to scour the beaches for more timber. We found very little, but just enough to keep the work going, enough to keep our spirits up.

Papa had finished carving Bull and Elephant by now and Maman was busy painting them. The turning gear, and the generator, were repaired and working again, and you could walk on half the floor, which Lorenzo and I did often, jumping up and down on it, singing "Sur le Pont d'Avignon," and imagining the carousel going around again. Best of all for Lorenzo was that Papa had been busy repairing and carving some of the flying pink flamingos from the frieze of the carousel. Six had been completed already. But we needed more wood badly, and it was becoming ever harder to find.

The morning the guns fired, Lorenzo and I were out riding Cheval with Henri, Lorenzo up in front wearing Henri's wide-brimmed hat as he loved to do, and me behind, clinging on. We had checked the horses and the bulls way out on the marshes and were coming home through the sheep pasture. It was summer. The skies were full of swallows, flying high, and everywhere out on the pink lakes there were egrets and flamingos.

When the guns went off, it was as if the world exploded around us. The ground shook far and wide, birds everywhere out over the marshes lifted as one great flock into the air. Cheval reared, tipped me off backward, and galloped away, leaving me lying there, shaken and bruised, my ears ringing and deafened. I saw Henri struggling to regain control of the horse, an arm round Lorenzo, trying to hold on to him at the same time. Somehow he managed it. The sheep had scattered in panic.

Henri came riding back to me, Lorenzo bewildered and crying. Henri gave me a hand up and we rode back to the farmyard. There was no one about. In the end, we found the others huddled together in the caravan. We sat there with them, unable to speak, with the ringing still in our ears, all of us hoping the guns would not fire again.

Lorenzo, though, had only one thing on his mind. "Flam flam, flam flam," he kept saying, pulling at Nancy's sleeve, and then taking my face in his hands, and turning me to look at him, to listen to him. "Flam flam, flam flam."

To calm him, I echoed his words again and again, as I knew he liked me to. But nothing I said, or Nancy said, seemed to make any difference. She sat him on her lap, blew raspberries on the back of his neck, and stroked his hair, which he usually loved, but there was no consoling him. He would not settle. He kept trying to get off her lap, to go outside. In the end, Nancy let him go. She thought he might perhaps be anxious about the fledglings in his shed, so she opened the door of the caravan for him and off he went.

"Go with him, Kezia," she told me.

I jumped down the steps and was about to run after him when I saw him standing there in the farmyard, quite still, rooted to the spot.

A German soldier was walking slowly toward him, limping. It was the giant Caporal. He was carrying a flamingo in his arms that was struggling to get away. There was blood on the feathers, on the wings, on the neck too. He was holding on to it only with the greatest difficulty. Maman was beside me now, Papa too, his arm on my shoulder.

Henri spoke up for us all. "We had an agreement," he told the Caporal. "No soldiers on the farm, you remember?"

"I remember, *monsieur*," replied the Caporal. "I am here only because I had to come. This morning, we tested our guns for the first time."

"We heard," Nancy told him.

"I am sorry to say there has been an accident, a casualty. We do not know how it happened, but all the flamingos, they took off and somehow this one was injured. So I came here to see you, to see your son."

The flamingo was struggling wildly in his arms.

"I hear it everywhere in the town, that Lorenzo has the

gift of healing, and I know that he loves flamingos. So I thought I must come here and bring him this wounded bird. They call him Flamingo Boy. Is this right?"

"Flam flam," murmured Lorenzo, walking up to the Caporal, "Flam flam." He reached out his hand, and with the tips of his fingers, stroked the flamingo on the neck, and then, leaning forward, breathed gently on her. The struggling stopped almost at once. He took the flamingo in his arms, gathering her close, then walked away toward his shed.

"The wing is broken, I think," said the Caporal. "I hope she will live, but she will not fly again, I am afraid."

Then I spoke up. "She will," I told him. "Lorenzo will mend the wing. Lorenzo will make her better."

"I hope you are right," said the Caporal. "And talking of mending things," he went on, "may I ask how work on your carousel is progressing? May I see it?" He did not wait for a reply, but walked past us, over to the barn, opened the doors and went in. I wanted to go after him, but Papa's hand was holding me back.

We stood there in silence until he emerged a short time later.

"You have done much good work," the Caporal said. "But I think you will need a lot more wood if you are to make the carousel what it was." He was looking straight at me now. "The floor of the carousel is coming on well. I see that you have found some good planks from somewhere."

"We found one in the canal," I said, but I knew I had said it too quickly. I did not sound convincing even to myself. I could feel Maman's eyes burning into me, but she said nothing.

"I have noticed that there is much that floats in these canals," the Caporal said. "Maybe you will find more if you go to look."

We could hear Lorenzo humming softly from inside his hospital shed, and moments later the sound of gentle honking.

"I brought the flamingo to the right place, I think," said the Caporal, smiling. "*Guten Tag*. I shall not bother you again."

He was about to turn and walk away when he thought again. "I just wanted to say something." He was talking now directly to Papa and Maman. "Monsieur and Madame

Charbonneau, if you will take my advice, you and your little girl will not leave the farm. Do not come into the town. It may be dangerous for you. The Milice, the police, they are guarding the roadblocks. They have been rounding up some of your people, Roma people, and taking them away. They have taken many Jews already. You may know this, but I thought I should tell you. So it is better not to be seen perhaps, not to be noticed. You are safer to stay here. Here you are hidden. You understand me?"

"What did he mean?" I asked Maman when he had gone. "Taking Roma people away? What did he mean? Where to? Is it like Madame Salomon?" She did not answer me. No one did. They simply looked at one another.

"It's just talk, nothing to worry about, Kezia," said Maman after awhile. "We told you, he told you, the Caporal. Here we are safe, so you must not worry."

And she said the same again that night when I asked her the same question. She kissed me good night, and held me tighter than she had ever done before. I could hear the flamingo honking from time to time from Lorenzo's hospital shed, and I could hear him humming in there. I longed to get out of bed and go to see him, but I knew I must not. But at least I could hear him, and his wounded flamingo. The humming and the honking lulled my fears, and in time lulled me to sleep. "

CHAPTER 23

Like a Miracle

"For days on end, Lorenzo hardly came out of his hospital shed. I knew he would invite me in when he was ready, and not before. He was silent and withdrawn whenever he came out. I would ask him about the flamingo, whether she was well enough yet for me to come and see her, but he would not reply. He would not even look at me. Even at meal times, he wanted to stay in the shed with his flamingo, but Nancy put her foot down.

"You have to eat, Lorenzo," she told him. "You must. You must eat for the flamingo. You need to be strong to do your healing." Nancy always had a way of saying the right thing to him. Even so, he was never happy about coming away and leaving his patient. He would walk up and down, nibbling unenthusiastically on his sausage. He had to finish every bit of it before Nancy would let him go back to his shed. It was as if the rest of us hardly existed. For days, he was like this. He lived only for the flamingo. His absence affected not just me, but all of us. It became like a cloud hanging over us that would not lift. Then one day it did, miraculously.

With Lorenzo shut away in his shed, I had taken to riding out with Henri on the farm whenever I could. Henri was the only one of us who seemed still to be much as he always had been, never morose or gloomy as the rest of us had become. He would just get on with the next job to be done, because it had to be done. I loved being out with him around the black bulls, driving them to new pastures, or riding in amongst the white horses and their foals, making sure none were walking lame, that the foals were fit and growing on well.

We were riding back one morning into the farmyard, Cheval trotting out as he always did when he was on his way back home, when we saw the most wonderful sight.

Lorenzo was walking across the yard toward the caravan, the flamingo at his side. The flamingo was stepping out strongly, wounded no longer, healed. Maman and Papa were standing there, watching them, and Nancy had come running out of the house. Lorenzo walked the flamingo around and around, clapping his hands with delight. The flamingo stayed close to him all the time, honking happily, both her wings outstretched. One moment Lorenzo and the flamingo were walking side by side, together, honking in harmony, moving in unison, then the next moment there seemed to be two flamingos.

"It is like a miracle," Nancy breathed. "A miracle." And so it seemed to all of us who were there to witness it. But that wasn't the only miracle that was to happen that day.

I was so happy to have Lorenzo back with me. He too made no secret either of his joy at our reunion, skipping along beside me, clapping his hands. We were never alone after that. The flamingo came with us, following us wherever we went. If she ever looked hesitant, or nervous, Lorenzo only had to honk gently and she would come running. I could see now that one of her wings would not stretch out quite as far as the other, that she was struggling to beat the air strongly, evenly, with both wings. I wondered then if the Caporal had been right, that the wing had been too seriously damaged, that she might never fly again.

I did not want to go back down the farm track toward Camelot, toward the concrete bunker and the guns and the soldiers. I did not want to be reminded of it. But one day Lorenzo insisted we go, dragging me along, and calling all the while to the flamingo to follow. We were coming ever closer to the bridge. We could see the hideous shape of the bunker, and hear the laughter of the soldiers. There was music playing, the soldiers singing. I saw them waiting by the wire, but they could not see us yet.

"No, Renzo," I said, taking both his hands and trying to persuade him to come away. "No, please, I want to go home. Come, Renzo, come." Then I had a lucky moment. I spotted an egret moving through the reeds beside the canal. "Grette!" I whispered, pointing it out to him. He had seen it. When I took his hand, he did not resist.

We followed the egret as it picked its way through the reeds along the shore of the canal, back toward home. We were almost there when Lorenzo stopped and crouched down to watch more closely. I did the same. The egret was busy feeding. The flamingo beside us was as still as we were.

That was when we noticed the water in the canal seemed to have changed color. It was no longer murky and gray, but brown, dark brown, the color of wood. I realized then that it wasn't just the color of wood. It *was* wood! The canal was full of planks, all jammed against one another, so tightly in places that it was more like a wooden floor that stretched across the canal, from one bank to the other. I could hardly believe what I was seeing.

"Twenty-nine," Lorenzo said. I counted. He was right, of course. Twenty-nine planks of wood were floating in the canal, some half submerged, some half hidden in the reeds.

I knew at once of course who had done this, and so did Lorenzo.

"Capo," he said, "Capo." I left Lorenzo and the flamingo there and ran home to the caravan. You cannot believe how fast I ran, how loud I was shouting, how garbled was the story I told them. I was back with Maman and Papa in a few minutes, with Honey and the cart. Papa had to wade into the canal waist-deep to reach all the planks, and float them over to our bank. Then Maman, Lorenzo, and I were dragging them through the reeds, hauling them up the bank and loading them onto the cart, the flamingo looking on, honking at us and flapping her wings.

When we had loaded every last one of the planks, Papa drove the cart home, Maman and me riding in the back, sitting on the pile of planks, Lorenzo following us up the farm track with the flamingo beside him. What a triumphant little cavalcade it was that Henri and Nancy must have seen coming into the yard.

We were all there in the barn later that morning, the planks laid out where they should go. Some were too short, some too long, but we could all see that there was enough wood now to finish the floor of the carousel. Standing there, gazing down at this bounty of timber, Maman and I knew, Lorenzo too, and everyone else suspected where the wood had come from, who had been our benefactor. His name was in all our minds, but no one dared speak it, not until Lorenzo did.

"Capo Capo," he said. "Capo Capo." He was telling everyone. He wanted the truth spoken.

Without Nancy, I do not think that Maman, Papa, and Henri would ever have accepted this gift from the enemy—for that, of course, is what it was: we all knew it.

"Well," said Nancy, standing on what would soon be the new floor of our carousel. "We have to make a choice, don't we? We can either take these planks, chop them up, and use them for firewood—but that would also be benefiting in a way from what the Caporal has given us. Or we could make a bonfire of the lot and watch it all go up in smoke, or we could see it simply as a gift of kindness and make good use of it. After all, we may not like the Germans one little bit, but they did not blow up our carousel. It was not an act of war, or of Occupation. A tree fell on it, and a French tree too. The big Caporal was there. He saw it in ruins. He wants to help us bring our carousel to life again. It is a gesture of kindness, of reconciliation. That is what I think."

"More important, he warned us about the Milice," Papa said, "told us to hide, to keep away from town, from the roads. Let us not forget that." To hear Papa speaking up for any German was a surprise, and a great relief to me. Papa

liked the giant Caporal, so it was all right for me to like him
too. That made me feel easier.

There was no need for any more discussion. They started
on the work to complete the floor of the carousel as soon
as the wood had dried out, and worked every evening late
into the night, sawing and planing, chiseling and hammering. I would listen from my bed in the caravan. It was music
to my ears. On one of those nights, I remember, I woke
crying from a nightmare, a nightmare of hammering in my
head that seemed to me like guns firing, louder and louder,
closer and closer. Maman was beside me, trying to calm
me, reassuring me that it was just Papa and Henri in the
barn, hammering the planks into place. Strange, *n'est-ce pas*,
Vincent, how we so often forget our dreams, but remember
our nightmares?

And *le flamand rose*, Lorenzo's flamingo? Well, she
became part of all our lives. She followed Lorenzo everywhere now, like a pink shadow. She was never allowed into
the farmhouse, though, so Lorenzo stayed outside with her
almost all the time. Only in the house at nighttime were
they ever separated. Nancy was adamant about it; she would

not have flamingo droppings and feathers all over the house. So, reluctantly and complaining, every evening Lorenzo would have to walk the flamingo back to the hospital shed for the night. She was not alone in there. There were several terrapins and two orphan flamingo fledglings to keep her company. But all the same she let us know how she felt about this enforced separation by honking regularly all night.

It was Lorenzo's miraculously recovered flamingo and the newly completed floor of the carousel that cheered us all. Forgotten were any past warnings of threat and danger. The Germans did not fire the guns again, no soldiers intruded onto the farm. The Milice did not come. We were left alone and in peace. Even the mosquitoes did not bother us so much. There were new foals and calves on the farm, plenty of fish in the canal, and Lorenzo was happy because the flamingos were breeding well out on the island in the middle of the lake. There were so many of them sitting on their nests that you could hardly see the island for flamingos.

All the time, progress on the carousel was gathering pace. The floor had made all the difference. Henri had straightened the damaged metal uprights that would support the roof. And Papa and Maman had now completed, much to Lorenzo's delight, ten of the flying pink flamingos that would soon adorn the crown of our new carousel. Henri and Nancy would come back from town on market days having sold everything they had taken in to sell. Food was becoming scarcer still these days, so demand was high.

With them, they brought good news, the best news there could be. There was more and more talk in the town that the Americans would be landing soon, that it could not be long. The war would not last forever. The Germans would be gone. Freedom was coming. 〞

CHAPTER 24

Flying Lessons

"But there was talk also of more and more acts of resistance and sabotage, and as a result the Germans and the brown-shirted Milice were becoming ever more aggressive and active. There were roadblocks everywhere. They were forever stopping people in the street, checking papers, and there were ever more arrests, more people being rounded up and taken away. And there were executions.

Not wanting to worry me, Henri and Nancy never told me any of this, but I found out anyway. Maman and Papa always tried not to talk of such things when I was about, but, when they whispered about it late at night in the caravan when they thought I was asleep, I listened in. Sleep and anxiety, they are not good bedfellows, Vincent, if you know what I mean.

But, during the day, we all had other things to think about. Before our eyes, something extraordinary was happening, something that helped banish all fears, all thoughts of war and Occupation, even of the dreaded Milice. Lorenzo was teaching his flamingo to fly, and I was helping him. I thought it was hopeless from the start. The flamingo was quite happy walking, happy running. It was obvious to me by now that she could not lift her right wing properly, and that unless she could she would never be able to fly.

When she did beat her wings, I could see it was to express joy and excitement, and her affection for Lorenzo. She was not even trying to fly, because she knew she could not. I knew she could not. Everyone knew she could not, except Lorenzo. He seemed to have no doubt that she would learn, that we could teach her.

He showed me what to do, which was to do what he did. We would walk, as flamingos do, stiff-legged, slowly, on either side of the flamingo down the farm track, in step with her, in time with her. Then we would begin to run, not fast, but rather with long, loping, unhurried strides, as a flamingo runs, arms moving as wings, beating slow at first, then faster, faster. And it almost worked too. Time and again, the flamingo almost became airborne, but never quite. A few wing beats was all she could ever manage.

After a few days, I was really beginning to believe that she now understood why we were doing all this, that she wanted to fly, was longing to fly. She was trying so hard. She was willing herself into the air. There were times when I really thought, as Lorenzo had always believed, that maybe she would do it.

We had help sometimes too, the best help we could have hoped for. A flock of flamingos would come flying in, honking overhead, and whenever they did I could see that our flamingo was making supreme efforts to lift herself, to fly as they did, but her damaged wing would never allow her to join them. Lorenzo didn't give up. Before every flying lesson, he would stand there with her, nose to beak, talking to her, encouraging her, stroking her neck, smoothing her wing feathers, humming to her.

I do not remember how long this went on, but it must

have been for weeks. I do remember the endless disappointments every time she tried but did not fly. One day she might improve, lift herself off the ground just a little, but she was never able to fly properly, no matter how much Lorenzo hoped and believed she would.

But he never lost hope, never lost belief. Maman and Papa thought as I did, that for all Lorenzo's belief, for all the flamingo's valiant efforts, it could never happen. In the privacy of the caravan, they could say such things, but outside, when they were watching these flying lessons, they would encourage Lorenzo all they could, clapping and cheering whenever the flamingo managed to lift herself, however briefly, off the ground. Nancy and Henri were the same. I could see from their faces that they too knew it was quite impossible. And all of us, I think, dreaded the final disappointment Lorenzo must one day have to face, when he too would have to accept that it could never happen, that his flamingo would never fly. But, as it turned out, we need not have worried.

It is strange and uncomfortable to have to say this, Vincent, but I honestly think the flamingo would never have flown at all without the Germans. Even now, I don't really like to admit that. *Mais c'est vrai*—it is true. Here's what happened. Lorenzo and I were yet again down the farm track by the canal, not far from Camelot. We had walked a little, run a little, keeping the flamingo between us as usual. That day she was showing no interest in flying at all. She had days like this, when I really thought she had had enough, that she was giving up. She was hardly bothering to beat her wings.

Then it happened. The guns fired, shattering the peace and quiet of the marshes, the thunderous blast of them so loud, so violent that we were thrown to the ground, or we threw ourselves down—I do not know which. When at last we looked up, Lorenzo's flamingo was no longer with us. Then I saw her, lifting up, working her wings frantically, then rhythmically, and at last becoming airborne, flying up to join the vast flock of birds above us, hundreds, thousands of them—egrets, storks, geese, and ducks amongst them— wheeling away over the marshes. Our flamingo was up there with them. She had gone! She had flown! Lorenzo and I were on our knees now, laughing and crying at the same time.

We touched foreheads. We jumped up and down in

joyous celebration, and then, clinging on to each other, we fell, and rolled over and over, down the bank and into the canal. Lorenzo stood up in the water, lifting his arms in the air in triumph. "Flam flam! Flam flam!" he cried.

I was standing there beside him, knee-deep in the canal, yelling out at the top of my voice: "Fly, flamingo, fly!"

And Lorenzo was echoing my words: "Fly, flamingo, fly!"

As we clambered back through the reeds together to the top of the bank, I looked up and saw boots, black boots, soldier's boots.

The giant Caporal was standing there. "The guns are very loud," he said. "It is not good for the ears. The flamingo, she is better?"

"She flew, she flew!" I cried, pointing up at the flock of flamingos circling overhead. "She is up there. Lorenzo taught her. I never thought she would fly again. Then the guns went off, and she flew."

"So the guns made her do it," said the Caporal, smiling broadly. "That makes me very happy. I am glad guns are good for something." He bent down to speak to us more confidentially. "And I think you found the wood in the canal?

Yes? That is good, very good. And the carousel, it will be finished one day?"

Lorenzo was on his feet now and clambering up to the top of the bank. The Caporal reached out and took his hand to help him. Lorenzo held on to his hand, and lifted it to his nose.

"Capo," he said. "Capo." Then, still holding his hand, he led the Caporal up the track toward the farmhouse.

As we walked, I asked the Caporal the question I had always wanted to ask him, but never quite dared, until now. "Did you hurt your leg?" I said.

"The war hurt my leg. The war hurts everything," he replied. "I was in Russia. I had frostbite. I lost some toes. It was cold in Russia, very cold. Snow, deep snow—not at all good for toes. Here you have mosquitoes, many mosquitoes. I prefer French mosquitoes to Russian snow. In Russia also my hair turned snow white. But it was not the snow that did that."

It was a strange conversation, but I have never forgotten it.

Lorenzo was not interested at all in what we were saying.

He was lost in wonder at the flocks of flamingos that filled the sky above us. I did not know if he, like me, was searching for his flamingo. I think it was enough to know she was up there with them.

"Fly, flamingo, fly!" He kept shouting it out again and again all the way up the farm track to the house. 🥢

CHAPTER 25

Trust

Kezia had closed her eyes, and I was wondering why.
"Vincent, I wonder if you have ever done this," she
said. "Have you ever shut your eyes sometimes, like I am
now, tight shut, and heard a memory, seen a memory? I only
have to do this, and I can still see this happening in my
head.

"The giant Caporal is there in the barn the
same day the flamingo flew, all of us with him,
and he is walking around and around on our newly finished
carousel floor, stamping on it, testing its strength, enjoying
his every step.

Then he stops and says this to us: "It is good to know that what is broken can always be mended, a flamingo wing, a carousel, and friendships too. I have two wishes. I want to be here long enough to see this carousel finished. I wish to see it turning once again in the town square, to hear the music, to see the children riding, laughing. But, on the other hand, my second wish is for this war to be over soon, even before the first of my wishes can happen. I would not be here to see the carousel, of course. But to know it will happen one day, that is enough for me."

None of us knew what to say, except Lorenzo. He used a word then that I had never heard him say before.

The Caporal was passing us on his way out of the barn when Lorenzo reached out and grasped his arm. As they touched foreheads, Lorenzo whispered to him: "Capo Capo. Trust, trust."

Now it was the Caporal who did not seem to know what to say. It wasn't until we followed him outside and he was walking away from us that he turned and spoke to us again.

"In German, it is *Vertrauen*. Trust. And remember what I said, about the Milice. Be watchful. Be safe."

Lorenzo would not let him go without a proper send-off. As the Caporal walked away, Lorenzo became flamingo, flamingo walking, flamingo dancing, taking off, flying, wings beating, neck stretched out, honking exultantly as he flew.

"Fly, flamingo, fly!" I cried, and we all echoed those words together.

I think it is likely we would have been left alone and untroubled, that no one would ever have bothered us, hidden away as we were out on the farm. It is ironic, but in a way it was the flamingos who were our downfall, who in the end brought the Milice to our door. Or rather, I should say, it was not the flamingos themselves, but their eggs.

Hardly anyone came to the farm these days, perhaps a neighbor with a sick calf for Lorenzo to heal, or a horse for Henri to shoe, though these were all good friends, trusted neighbors. But it was April, springtime on the farm, the time when all of us had to be especially on our guard against egg-robbers. This was the month the flamingos gathered on the island, crowding together, and laid their eggs, and bred their chicks.

The egg-robbers would come in the early mornings or at dusk, and wade out over to the pink lakes, to the breeding islands, to steal the eggs from under the sitting flamingos. It happened every year—occasionally, as I told you, Vincent, it still does. So, morning and evening, someone had to be there on lookout.

Usually, it was Henri and Lorenzo together out there, watching the island, sitting on the upturned rowing boat by the lakeside. Nancy thought the egg-robbers might not come this year. There were still roadblocks everywhere, and a curfew too. No one would risk it, she said. Henri, though, was quite sure they would come. People were going hungry now in the Camargue under the Occupation. There was very little food, and what there was was very expensive too. The Germans were taking for themselves all the food they could get. So there were plenty of people trying to survive on very little, especially in the towns, but also in the countryside around about. Just three flamingo eggs made a good meal for a family. So flamingo eggs would be especially sought after this year, he said. Sadly, it was Henri who turned out to be right.

It was the first and only argument I ever heard between Nancy and Henri. He was hammering away at his forge, shaping new horseshoes for Cheval. Cheval was standing there, wreathed in smoke, ears back, hating it but putting up with it—Cheval, so unlike Honey, put up with everything. Lorenzo and I heard them arguing between the echoing hammer blows, and listened unseen from inside the hospital shed.

"And I tell you, they will come this year whether we like it or not," Henri was saying. "And I say we should let them come and take the eggs. There are people starving. They need the food, Nancy—you know that. The flamingos will breed again next year. Who are more important, people or flamingos?"

"Flamingos!" Nancy retorted. "Do flamingos make wars? Do they make guns? Do they make slaves of people? Do they take gypsy people away, and Jews like Madame Salomon, and put them in camps, or worse, because they are different? No, flamingos live only to feed and to fly, to lay their eggs and breed. You know that every year we see fewer of them, and there are fewer islands where it is safe for them to raise their young. The foxes take them. The wild boar take them. The badgers take them. And if we take their eggs as well, steal them and eat them, what chance do they have? And, anyway, what would Lorenzo think if he knew we were not out there morning and evening, protecting their eggs, keeping the thieves away? We have always done it, every year. He does it—we all do it!"

Lorenzo had heard enough. He left the shed, and I followed. He walked right up to his father, and said in a trembling voice: "Fly, flamingo, fly, Papa. Fly, flamingo, fly."

Then he took him firmly by the hand and led him away from his anvil across the farmyard to the edge of the lake. There the flamingos were, crowded onto their island, in their hundreds, incubating their eggs. Lorenzo sat down on the upturned fishing boat at the edge of the lake and pulled Henri down beside him, holding his arm fast.

"Renzo stay. Papa stay."

There was no more argument. Early every morning and evening two of us were always there, sitting on the upturned boat, watching the nesting site for intruders, whether fox or badger or wild boar or human. The water level, Nancy told me, was high enough in the lakes this year to keep most predators away, but it was still shallow enough for the egg-robbers to be able to wade out. And come they did, not at dusk or dawn as everyone was expecting they might, but in broad daylight.

The flamingos raised the alarm themselves, lifting off in a cacophony of urgent honking. Maman spotted the thieves first from the steps of the caravan. Half a dozen men were wading out across the lake, some of them already on the island. By the time we were all there at the lakeside, Henri with his rifle in hand, the egg-robbers were already busy raiding the nests, filling their sacks with eggs, while above them the flamingos wheeled and soared, helpless to do anything about it. But we could.

The egg-robbers ignored our shouting, but Henri's rifle was enough to make them pay attention. He fired one shot in the air. That stopped them collecting. The next shot sent them scurrying in a panic off the island, splashing through the lake, making their escape, some leaving their sacks behind them, all except one, and I recognized him. He was from town, the father of Bernadette, my old tormentor at school. He stood his ground, sack over his shoulder, and was hurling abuse at Henri and Papa as they came wading out toward the island.

Lorenzo and I wanted to go with them, but Maman and Nancy held us back. Across the water, we couldn't hear every hateful word he was yelling at them, but we could hear enough.

"We know about you, Henri Sully! You have gyppos for friends! You wait, I have a brother in the Milice, and I promise you he will hear of this!" Henri fired another shot into the air as they neared the island. "You will regret this, Henri Sully, I promise you!" Then he turned, jumped down into the water and waded away to join his friends on the far shore where they stood, shaking their fists, yelling expletives and curses at us.

By then we had joined Henri and Papa on the island, and were already busy emptying their discarded sacks and putting the eggs back onto the nests. Above us the flock of flamingos circled, waiting for us to complete our task and be gone. Their triumphant honking sounded to us like a battle cry of victory and freedom. We had seen off the enemy, retaken the island and saved at least some of the eggs. We were soaked through and chilled to the bone by the time we got home afterward, but the raiders had been repulsed, the flamingos were back on their island, and we were exultant. We should not have been. **"**

CHAPTER 26

They Will Be Back

"Henri was sitting there, silent and deep in thought, as we laughed and celebrated our famous victory. When he did speak, he had words of warning for us, and for Maman and Papa and me especially.

"They will be back," he said, "and next time I do not think they will come only for the eggs. You heard him. That man has family in the Milice. They will come."

Henri looked up at Papa and Maman. "Until now, they may have forgotten you. Not anymore. If they didn't know before, they know where you are now. There is nowhere we can hide you, not here, not near the house. But there is the fisherman's hut out on the marshes—it hasn't been used for years. I have sheltered cows and calves in there from time to time. The roof leaks, but it is shelter. In town, they don't even know such a place exists. You'd be safe there for awhile. You could hide away and no one would find you. And we could bring you everything you need. It is all I can think of."

"And the carousel?" said Papa. "Who will look after the carousel?"

"We will," Nancy told him. "We will, and when the Americans come, and it cannot be long now, you can come back, and we will finish it together."

"We will take you out there in the morning," said Henri, "but early, before dawn, so no one sees us. Tonight you must pack what you need. And take blankets; the nights might be cold out there."

That is what we were doing that same evening. Lorenzo was shadowing me, holding my hand whenever he could. He knew well enough what was happening, and he did not want me to go. After awhile, he wanted to be alone with me, I could tell. He led me down to the lake and we sat silent on the upturned boat, looking out to the island.

We had no words, until he said: "Three hundred forty-one."

That was the moment we heard the sound of a car, several of them, coming up the farm track, and coming fast. Three cars were pulling up outside the farmhouse. Everything happened so quickly after that. Lorenzo lifted the boat by the bow. I knew at once what he wanted me to do. I crawled in under and he lowered the boat over me. I cowered there in the dark, terrified. I could hear what was going on, all the shouting, and the breaking down of doors. Lorenzo was sitting on the boat now above my head. I could feel the boat rocking back and forth, hear him moaning and humming. I heard the splintering of glass, and raucous laughter, then the sound of footsteps running toward us.

"Two!" someone was shouting. "We've only got two of them. He said there were three gyppos out here. There's a girl too, he said. She's got to be hereabouts somewhere." And then his voice was coming closer. "You! Idiot boy! Flamingo Boy! The gyppo girl, where is she?"

"Fly, flamingo, fly," Lorenzo murmured again and again,

rocking so hard now that the boat was creaking above my head. "Fly, flamingo, fly."

"He's loopy in the head. Daft as a bloody brush!" It was another voice from farther away. "Come on, Paul, we've got two of them. That'll do. The gyppo girl's probably run off into the marshes. She won't last long out there on her own. Look, they're burning the caravan. Gyppos, dirty beggars they are—they live like lousy rats, they do!"

I did not see the caravan burning. I smelled the smoke, and imagined the rest. Imagining is sometimes worse, Vincent. I did not see them manhandling Maman and Papa into the cars, but I knew it was happening. I only heard car doors slamming, more shouting, and the sound of the cars driving away. Then there was nothing but sobbing, and the distant crackling of flames. I thought it was all over, that they were gone. But then I heard more footsteps coming close, running footsteps, and I knew they were coming for me too. I curled myself into a ball in the darkness, biting my lip to stop myself from crying out.

"Renzo, have you seen Kezia?" It was Nancy's voice. "Did you see where she went?" Lorenzo was rocking more violently now. I could hear the fear in his humming. "It's all right, Renzo, all right," Nancy said. She was sitting down beside him, on the boat, right above me. "They've gone," she went on. "But Kezia, we can't find her, Lorenzo. They didn't take her. She's around here somewhere. She must be. She can't have gone far."

"Zia Zia!" Lorenzo said. He was tapping the side of the boat, trying to tell her. Moments later, the bow of the boat was being lifted. I crawled out. Both of them were holding me then. I buried my head in their arms, clung to them, not wanting to look up and see the caravan in flames, not wanting to remember what I knew had happened.

When at last I did dare to lift my head and look, I saw Henri throwing buckets of water on what was left of the caravan, and he was not alone. The Caporal was there, two of his soldiers with him, all of them trying desperately to put the fire out. But it was hopeless—I could see that at once. The caravan was burning from end to end, the flames roaring up into the sky, smoke billowing out over the farmyard, showers of sparks landing all around us.

Terrible though it was to see my home burning, all I

could think of was Maman and Papa. I realized they had taken Maman and Papa away, but still I looked for them everywhere, called for them, screamed for them. It was as fruitless as throwing buckets of water onto those flames, but I could not help myself. We stood there and watched as more soldiers came rushing up the farm track to try to pump water from the lake onto the fire. It was all too late. My home had been destroyed. There was little left but ashes, and Maman and Papa had been taken from me. Nancy's strong arms were still holding me, but she could not hold back my tears.

The Caporal was coming toward us with Henri, both of them with eyes reddened from the smoke, their faces smeared.

I asked the Caporal through my tears: "Where have they taken my *maman* and *papa*?"

"I do not know," he told me, "but I will find out. Believe me, I did not know this would happen. We are no angels, but to do this, to do this . . . this is shameful." He came closer to me and crouched down. "I will see that no harm comes to them. You have to believe me, to trust me."

"Trust, Capo," Lorenzo echoed. "Capo, trust, trust."

The Caporal stood up, wiping his face with the back of his hand. "I can promise you this. From now on, my soldiers will make sure no one comes past the gun emplacement onto your farm. We shall block the road. No more Milice will get through. But there are other ways to reach the farm, across the marshes. So it is best from now on, I think, to keep the little girl out of sight. It will not be for long. The Americans will be here soon—that is what we hear, and I am sure it is true. Then this war will quickly be over. I can go home, and your *maman* and *papa* can come home too."

"But where are my *maman* and *papa*?" I asked him again.

The Caporal hesitated before replying. "There are places where they take Roma people."

"But why have they taken them, Caporal?" said Nancy. "That I think is a more difficult question for you to answer."

"I know the answer to that, *madame*," the Caporal replied. "It is because the world has gone mad, and it is we who have made it mad. But when all this madness is over, and it will be soon, you and your family and your carousel can help mend the world, help put right the wrongs we have done."

He walked away then, taking his soldiers with him, leaving the ashes smoldering behind him. Through the drifting smoke out in the field, we saw Honey intent on her grazing, as if nothing had happened. We smiled at that, and then at one another. I needed a smile, Vincent, you cannot imagine how much I needed a smile at that moment. ""

Kezia took a deep breath then that became a long sigh, as she gazed sadly into the fire. "I can never look into a fire without remembering," she said, and remained silent for awhile. I thought she might be going to find some reason or other not to go on with the story. But, when she lifted her head, I could see she was ready to continue, that she wanted to finish it. She wanted to tell it all. I felt then for the first time that this was a story she was anxious to pass on, that she wanted me to hear, and that for reasons I did not know, and still do not know, she had chosen me.

*

"**T**he night of the caravan fire was the first time I ever slept in this house, Vincent. I slept with them upstairs, in the room where I still sleep all these years later. Four in the bed we were that night, all of us huddled together against the world. But sleep came to none of us. It was not only Lorenzo who kept me awake, as he rocked himself, as he hummed and muttered to himself that night. I wouldn't have slept anyway. I kept trying not to think of Maman and Papa, of what might be happening to them, of where they were. If it was a camp they had been taken to, as I think I remembered someone saying, then that would not be so bad. A camp was not so bad. I was hoping that, wherever they were, they would meet up with Madame Salomon, that they could all look after one another. I knew Madame Salomon would be as kind to them as she had been to me. In the middle of the night though came my darkest thoughts, that I would not see them ever again.

I prayed to Saint Sarah, tried to pray as I had done when I was little, Maman kneeling with me in front of her icon in the caravan, with the candle burning beside it. But Saint Sarah could not comfort me because I could not believe in her as I had then. All the same, I kept praying to her, night after night, more in hope than in faith. Thinking back, she kept my hopes alive. And I am still trying to work out, Vincent, when hope becomes faith, and what faith is without hope. **"**

CHAPTER 27

A Light in the Darkness

"The Caporal was as good as his word. Nancy told me the next day that a roadblock had gone up across the farm track just beyond the bridge and the gun emplacement, so no one at all could come that way onto the farm and trouble us. Of course, I never saw this roadblock, confined as I was to the house all day and every day.

We did as the Caporal had told us. We laid low, kept ourselves to ourselves. Nancy and Henri made sure I stayed out of sight inside the farmhouse. I hoped against hope that the Milice would not come searching for me. I lived in dread of the sound of a car pulling up outside, and the knock on the door. Nancy tried to reassure me again and again that I must not worry, that the Caporal would do all he could to look after us, and that anyway she was sure the Milice would not be bothered to come hunting after one little Roma girl who, so far as they knew, could be anywhere now out on the marshes.

Nancy still left the farm once a week to set up the stall in the market, because she had to.

"We have to live," she said. When she wasn't with me in the house, Lorenzo would come and be with me all day, and not just, I felt, to keep me company, but to look after me, almost as if I was one of his flamingo fledglings. He would sit beside me, reaching out from time to time to touch my hair or my cheek and humming to me as he hummed to them. Henri went about the farmwork as usual, unperturbed, resolute in his determination to carry on. They were all trying to make me feel safe, but I knew I was not.

I suppose I lived much as you have had to live, Vincent—until recently that is—shut up in this house, unable to venture out at all. How I longed to be outside again, to run free with Lorenzo. I spent long hours at the bedroom window upstairs, gazing out through broken shutters over the marshes, watching the flamingos and egrets coming and going. Nancy had closed the shutters downstairs and forbade me from ever opening them. A face in any window at the wrong time, she warned me, and I could be discovered. I did have somewhere to hide. If the worst came to the worst, if they did come to search the house, Henri had made a false bottom inside the big blanket chest in the bedroom. I was to crawl in there, lie down and stay there until it was safe to come out. They made me practice hiding in there. I hated doing it, but I knew it had to be done.

Nancy would never let me spend too long alone in the house. She knew how anxious I was, every waking hour, about the Milice coming again, and about Maman and Papa. So she kept me busy, working with her in the kitchen, helping her make the sheep's cheese, sorting the herbs for market, salting the fish, and of course there were my lessons. I still had my lessons with her, every day without fail. It was difficult to concentrate, but I think those lessons were the saving of me, for it was during these long weeks that I began to read on my own, for myself, not only to read to Lorenzo, but now for my own pleasure too.

They did not have many books in the house, but the few they had I read again and again. I loved stories of travel and adventure, especially Alexandre Dumas's *The Three Musketeers* and *The Man in the Iron Mask*, and then there were Jules Verne's *Around the World in Eighty Days* and *Twenty Thousand Leagues Under the Sea*. In these stories, I could escape from the four walls of the farmhouse for awhile, and escape all the fears that so easily overwhelmed me about Papa and Maman, and the Milice, about having to hide in the darkness of the blanket chest if they came.

As time went by, Nancy constantly tried to dispel my anxiety as best she could. The Milice would have long forgotten all about me by now, she said. As for Maman and Papa, I had to trust the Caporal. Remember how much he had helped us out with the timber for the carousel? Hadn't he told us he would find out where Maman and Papa had been taken, to do all he could to see they were safe? He would do what he had promised, she was sure of it.

But the days passed and the weeks passed and there was still no word from the Caporal. I could not help thinking sometimes that he had abandoned us altogether, that he was not to be trusted, and that anyway he could not protect me from the Milice, whatever he had promised. After all, they had come and taken Maman and Papa away, hadn't they? He hadn't been able to stop them then. And weren't they all on the same side anyway, the Milice and the Germans, the Caporal too? Hadn't Papa warned us that the Caporal wore the uniform of the Nazis, the enemy, the invader, the occupier, and that we should never forget that?

Nights were the worst to endure. After my prayers to Saint Sarah, I would lie awake for endless hours, longing for the comfort of sleep, but listening for the sound of a car, for heavy footsteps outside, for the knock on the door. Fears piled on fears so, by the time morning came, despite all the praying, I had often lost all hope.

In the end, it wasn't Nancy, or keeping busy, or the reading, or the praying that brought me the greatest comfort: it was Lorenzo. We found we needed each other in these dark times more than ever. The terrible day when the Milice had come and invaded his world, the day he hid me under the boat and saved me became for Lorenzo like a recurring living nightmare. The memory of the caravan on fire haunted him. He could not put it out of his head. I think it haunts him still, which is why I never speak of any of this when he is around, Vincent.

He would sometimes have panic attacks. Out of nowhere, all of a sudden, he could become frantic. He would start banging his head with his hands, or even hitting his forehead against the wall, if we did not stop him in time. He raged about the place, wide-eyed with agitation. I was the one he often ran to when he was having one of his fits. It was me that Nancy and Henri turned to now to help calm him down, to comfort and console, to bring him back to himself. I would hold his face in my hands, talk to him softly about Camelot or flamingos, sing "Sur le Pont d'Avignon" to him, and in time we would be touching foreheads, and I knew the worst was over. He would cry then, holding on to me so tight and for so long that I thought he might never let go. It was strange, but, in comforting him, he was comforting me just as much.

We would often end up side by side, on that sofa you're sitting on now, Vincent, with me reading him his Arthur stories over and over again. This seemed to transport him to his Camelot, to how it had been during the happy times we had had there together. I was his "Guin Guin" again, and he was "Art Art, *roi, moi!*" The anger and pain and the panic were forgotten as suddenly as they had appeared, and he would be himself again, leaping to his feet to slay another dragon. "Agon agon!" would be his victory chant, and Nancy, Henri, and I would all applaud his knightly courage. But we knew there would be a next time, a new attack of panic that would suddenly overwhelm him, and for that we had always to be prepared.

Perhaps it was because he felt everything so intensely that Lorenzo understood the feelings of others so well, human or animal. Whenever I was filled up with sadness, and near to despair again—as I often was, thinking that Maman and Papa were lost to me forever—I would find him at my side, humming to me, my hand held tight in his. So, leaning on each other, comforting each other, the weeks passed slowly, ever more slowly, but still there was no news of Maman and Papa.

But then came a day of great hope, a light in the darkness,

a day of joy—and where there is joy there is comfort—*c'est vrai*, Vincent? And it was Henri who brought me such unexpected joy. For days on end, I hardly ever saw him. He was out in the fields every hour of the day, sometimes with Lorenzo, sometimes with Nancy. Lorenzo, I noticed, often came back from working with him out on the farm, clapping his hands with excitement, and would caper about the room, giggling and laughing.

Nancy seemed to know what it was all about. She said nothing, neither did Lorenzo, and neither did Henri. Sometimes I saw looks and surreptitious smiles passing amongst the three of them. There was definitely something they were not telling me, something confidential, a family secret of some kind, I supposed. Henri would come in late, exhausted, say little or nothing during supper, sit in his chair by the fire, and be fast asleep almost at once.

On this particular evening, Henri came in even later than usual—it was already dark outside—but he didn't come and sit down as he always did. He stood by the open door in his dirty clogs, and said, "Come, I have something to show you—you too, Kezia, especially you."

"No, Henri," Nancy said. "You heard what the Caporal said. He told us to always keep Kezia inside, to keep her hidden, never to let her go out." I felt she was playacting as she was saying this, but had no idea why.

"Our Caporal has done much for us," Henri told her, "and I am very grateful to him. But I do not take orders from a German soldier, even him. It's safe enough in the dark for Kezia. No one will see. Come." He was playacting too.

It was wonderful to be outside again, despite the mosquitoes. Lorenzo was holding my hand tight as we followed Henri across the yard toward the barn. He was skipping up and down, unable to contain himself, pulling at me all the time to come faster.

"Secret, Zia Zia, secret," he kept whispering, putting his finger to his lips. I could see lamplight flickering inside as we approached the open doors.

We walked in. In the center of the barn there were enough lamps lit for me to be able to see well enough. And what a wonderful sight it was! I could hardly believe my eyes. The carousel had grown, grown into itself, into what it was, into what it was going to be. It was not just a floor anymore. The uprights were in place, the roof was on, and, best of all, the frieze of flying pink flamingos was complete. The carousel was wearing its coronet of flamingos once again!

"Secret secret! Fly, flamingo, fly!" Lorenzo cried, and set off around the carousel, running like a flamingo, then flying, wings beating, honking through his laughter as happy as I'd ever seen him.

There were no rides on the carousel—none of the animals were in place as yet—so the floor was empty. But what had once been nothing but a wreck and a ruin had been transformed. We had our carousel again, not complete, not yet as it had once been, but it was our carousel. As if to prove it, Lorenzo jumped up onto the floor and beckoned me to join him. Then I saw Henri bending over the cranking handle, and turning it, just as Papa had done. We were moving! We were turning! The carousel was working!

But better still was to come. From the darker depths of the barn beyond the lamplight, I heard music playing. The tune of "Sur le Pont d'Avignon" was filling the barn. Through my tears, I could just make out Nancy now at the barrel organ. Lorenzo was singing along, shouting along, loud and tuneless as usual. Then we were all singing, and Lorenzo and I were flamingo dancing too, and singing our hearts out at the same time. I sang out loud for Maman and Papa, willing them safe, willing them home to see their carousel again, to see me again. **"**

CHAPTER 28

A Knock at the Door

"**I** did not want the carousel to stop when it did— I did not want it to stop ever. When the music stopped also, Henri said: "Well, what do you think? We have all been working on it as hard as we could, Kezia, so that when your *maman* and *papa* come back—and they will, soon, you will see—all they will have to do is to finish carving and painting the rest of the rides. We will find the wood we need from somewhere. Your *papa* made two already, and your *maman* painted them—you see them, over there in the corner? They are waiting for them to come back and make the others. And then your carousel will be ready."

Lorenzo was tugging at Henri's arm. He was trying to

remind him to say something, I was sure of it. "Capo, Papa. Capo Capo."

Nancy and Henri were looking at each other, unsure what to say, hesitating. I knew at once then that they had news of Maman and Papa.

"What about the Caporal?" I asked. "Have you seen him? Has he seen Maman and Papa? Are they well? Where are they?" They did not answer for some time.

Fear of the unknown, fear of the worst crept through me, and chilled me to the bone. "What?" I said, "What do you know?"

It was Nancy who told me. "It is mostly good news, Kezia. Don't worry. The Caporal came to see Henri today. He has found out where your *maman* and *papa* are. He has even been to see them. They are in a camp in the Camargue, not too far away, at Saliers. There are many Roma people there, so they are among friends."

"Camp?" I said. "What sort of camp? Is Madame Salomon there?"

Henri answered, but only after awhile, and I could see it was because Nancy did not want to. "I don't think so. It is a kind of prison camp, Kezia," he said. "But the Caporal said they are well enough. He said they send you all the love they have, and that they will be home to see you soon. They know you are safe with us."

"You will see them soon, Kezia, soon," Nancy said, her arms around me. "All will be well, you will see." I believed her because I wanted so much to believe her.

"You believe me?" she said.

"I do!" I cried. "I do!"

Then Henri was turning the cranking handle again, jolting the carousel into motion, so that Lorenzo and I lost our balance and fell over. I abandoned myself to hope, to hope of joy to come, and we lay there clutching each other and giggling. It was the best ride I ever had on our carousel. No Elephant, no Dragon, no Horse, just Lorenzo and me rolling around on the floor, Nancy playing the music on the barrel organ, and Henri turning us faster and faster. I lay there with Lorenzo, all my worries forgotten. Maman and Papa were alive and well, the Americans were coming, the war would soon be over, and Maman and Papa would come home again. They would, they would! All would be well.

As I lay there on the floor of the carousel, I remember I closed my eyes and thanked Saint Sarah, in whom I wanted so much to believe. I prayed to her fervently. I thanked her again and again, out loud this time, with Lorenzo gripping my hand. I prayed to her for the war to end, soon, very soon, because I knew the lives of Maman and Papa and Madame Salomon depended on it. I clung to Nancy's words, held the image of the icon of Saint Sarah in my head, and spoke Nancy's words to myself at night over and over again. "You will see them soon, Kezia, soon. All will be well, you will see."

But the war did not end. Instead, Nancy brought back from town on market days stories of resistance fighters—*maquisards* she called them—blowing up factories and train lines and convoys of German trucks. They were becoming more and more active everywhere. The Germans and the Milice were ever more nervous, ever more vicious and vengeful. I overheard between Nancy and Henri many hushed conversations about reprisals and public executions.

I remember Henri saying once: "We must be careful. The Germans, the Milice, they are like wounded animals now. They know they have lost. They are cornered, and cornered animals are always at their most dangerous."

I dared not ask about all of this, not just because they would know I had been eavesdropping on their private conversations and they would be upset, but because the more I heard the less I wanted to know. Every time they spoke of those things, I felt the threat of danger coming ever closer to us. They were always watchful, reminding me again and again never to show myself, not to look out of the windows at all, upstairs or downstairs. Our greatest fear, an unspoken fear, was to hear the sound of car tires crunching to a halt outside the house, to hear the dreaded knock at the door.

So, when the knock at the door did come, I was not surprised. But I was terrified. We were all upstairs in the same bed as usual. I was woken by something. I thought it was the light of dawn at first. The birds were singing, the flamingos joining in the chorus. Then I heard the squeal of brakes outside, the sound of a slamming car door. My heart filled with terror. We were all awake by now and sitting up. Then came the knocking on the door, urgent, insistent, and someone was shouting in German. For just a few moments,

I held the hope that this was only a nightmare, my worst nightmare, that I would wake up, and would realize it was not happening, that it would all go away. But the knocking had become a pounding.

"Open up! Open up!"

Within moments, I had jumped into the blanket chest, and was lying there in the blackness, the false bottom and the blankets above me. I heard the lid close.

"I'll go," I heard Henri say.

"No," Nancy told him firmly. "We go together, Lorenzo too. Stay still, Kezia," she whispered. "Stay still." They left the room and I heard them go downstairs. I heard the bolts being drawn back, the door open, then Henri's voice.

"Caporal," he said. "What are you doing here?" The blanket chest was right above the front door. I could hear every word.

My first thoughts—and I am still ashamed to say this—was that the Caporal had betrayed us, that his friendship had been false all along.

Papa had warned me, warned all of us. "They all wear the uniform. Never forget that," he had said.

"You must get dressed," the Caporal was saying. "You are leaving. I will escort you, take you somewhere safe."

"What is going on, Caporal?" Nancy asked.

"Capo Capo!" Lorenzo was saying. I could hear the affection in his voice, the trust, and I was ashamed of myself for doubting him then. It was not easy to push up the false bottom above me, but I did. I pulled aside the blankets, opened the top of the chest, climbed out, and ran downstairs.

The Caporal smiled when he saw me. "I wondered where you were," he said. He looked at his watch then. "I have little time to explain. In less than one hour, we are going to blow up the gun emplacement. There will be a big explosion, a very big explosion, and we do not know what damage will be done to the house, but it is certain the windows will be shattered, and who knows what else. It is too dangerous for you to stay. I will drive you to the end of the farm, as far away as possible."

"Why?" Nancy asked. "Why are you blowing it up?"

"The Americans have landed, sooner than we thought, and farther up the coast, not at all where we expected. So the guns are useless. The Americans will be here soon enough. We are destroying all our guns, all our sea defenses, everything we cannot take with us, so nothing can be used against us. And, once it is done, we will be moving out, and you will have your peace again. I hope the same for myself and my men one day, but that is less certain, I think."

I needed to ask him myself. "My *maman* and *papa*?" I said. "You saw them? They are in a camp?"

"Yes, Kezia," he said. "I will not pretend to you they are in a pleasant place. I will not pretend they are happy. No one can be happy in such a place; no one is happy behind wire fences. But they looked well and they are strong and determined. I have spoken to the people there, to the Commandant also. The Charbonneau Carousel is well known—the Commandant himself had seen and much admired it. Do not worry about your *maman* and *papa*. They will come home to you, Kezia, but when I cannot tell." He was more formal again suddenly, more the soldier. "Now you must hurry. Get dressed. There is no time to lose."

Within minutes, we were all dressed and ready to go, and the Caporal was driving us away, Henri beside him in the front seat, giving him directions as to where to take us. I could hear little of what they were saying over the sound of the engine, over the rattling and bumping as we drove down the farm track alongside the lake. In the early morning light, I could see flamingos out there watching us as we were watching them. Until he saw them, Lorenzo had been quite bewildered and upset by all that had gone on, but not anymore. His hands, I remember, were flat against the window as we passed by the flamingos, his face pressed to the glass.

The Caporal drove us as far as the track went, to the ruined fisherman's hut at the end of the farm. I had been there once before with Henri on Cheval. Here we all got out. Standing there outside the fisherman's hut, none of us seemed to know what to say, except Lorenzo. He went up to the Caporal, and they touched foreheads.

"Capo Capo," he whispered. "Trust, trust."

"Trust," the Caporal echoed.

Then Henri said what was in all our hearts to say, "Get home safely, Caporal."

"Why?" Nancy asked him then. "Why have you helped us so much?"

"Before I was a Caporal, before I went to Russia," the

Caporal replied, "before I came to France, before I had white hair, I was Willi Brenner from Tübingen. I am a teacher—I was a teacher. Children were my life. And I had a boy of my own, eleven years old, Hans, but the bombs killed him a year ago. He was a happy boy, the light of our lives. Hans—I know he would have loved your carousel. After I heard he had died, I wanted only to save children. *Auf Wiedersehen, meine Freunde.*"

He got in his car and was about to leave when he seemed to remember something.

"I had forgotten this, Kezia," he said, handing me a small envelope. "I found it that day in the ashes of your caravan. I picked it up, put it in my pocket, then forgot about it. It is yours, I think."

I opened the envelope. It was only a fragment of something, and it was scorched, but it was instantly recognizable to me as I turned it over in my hand. It was the icon of Saint Sarah.

To this day, I was not sure why I did what I did next. I think it was because my heart was so full of gratitude for all this man had done for us. I gave it back to him.

"You keep it, Capo," I said. "Saint Sarah and you, you have both looked after us. Now she will look after you. Keep it."

He took it, said not a word and drove away. At once, I regretted giving it to him. But then I regretted my regretting. Somehow I knew deep down that he needed it now more than I did. It was the moment I think that my belief became stronger than my hope.

We sat in the dilapidated fisherman's hut, wrapped in our blankets, and waited. It was a fragile shelter, but it was at least some shelter from the driving rain, and from whatever was to happen. The waiting seemed to go on forever. We hardly spoke. Lorenzo rocked back and forth, humming, but he was not frantic, not panicking as I feared he might be. He was humming his favorite tune, and ours too. Soon, sitting there, arms linked, we were all humming along to "Sur le Pont d'Avignon." And waiting, waiting.

I have never in my life known a sound like it. It may have happened far away, but it was as if it was right above us, all around us. It did not just fill our ears and heads, it shook the ground under our feet. The door of the hut blew open. Every bird for miles around seemed to be airborne at once, filling the sky with their cries, with their honking.

"Fly, flamingo, fly," Lorenzo moaned. "Fly, flamingo, fly." I knew it was a prayer for all his beloved flamingos.

I held him close to me, forehead to forehead, and repeated his prayer with him. "Fly, flamingo, fly; fly, flamingo, fly," I whispered.

Walking home afterward through the marshes, through the fields of black bulls and white horses, I could see Lorenzo was searching the fields and lakes all around us, but we saw no wounded birds, not one. They were all still up there, soaring above us, the honking of the flamingos singing out in a great and joyous chorus. They had survived. So had we. "

CHAPTER 29

Free at Last! Free Again!

"When we got back to the farmhouse, we discovered that almost every window had been broken; shattered glass lay everywhere. The chimney had been blown off and had fallen down through the roof. How right the Caporal had been to get us out of harm's way. There were dozens of roof tiles scattered about, like fallen autumn leaves, around the walls of the house. Pieces of shattered concrete littered the farmyard—some as big as rocks—and down the farm track a cloud of smoke and dust still lingered everywhere. It was in the air, in our lungs. Nancy could not stop coughing. She gave me a handkerchief to hold over my mouth.

Cheval was careering around his field, neighing in his terror. Henri ran over and caught him, and was holding him by his halter, breathing into his nose to calm him, just as Lorenzo might have done. Honey was in the same field, grazing contentedly as usual. She barely lifted her head to look at us. The grass all around was not green anymore, but gray with dust. Nancy had gone straight into the house by this time to see what damage had been done inside. My ears were still reverberating from the sound of the explosion. I was standing there, numbed, bewildered, unable to gather my thoughts, when I suddenly realized I was alone. Lorenzo had wandered off. I knew at once where he must have gone.

He was crossing the wooden bridge by the time I caught up with him. There were no soldiers to be seen. Everywhere I walked I saw the debris of the explosion strewn about on the farm track, in the canal, in the stream, in among the rushes. I clung tight with both hands to the rail as I crossed the bridge—or what was left of it. Only a couple of planks were still intact, and I wasn't at all sure they would be strong enough to hold my weight. I stepped across tentatively, calling for Lorenzo all the time. But if he was in the castle he was not replying.

I was in the courtyard, calling for him, looking for him, when his head suddenly rose up from behind our rock in the middle of the courtyard.

"Lot Lot!" he cried, and then he was up there, up on the rock, arms raised in the air. "Guin Guin. *Roi, moi!*" His whole being was wreathed in laughter, and he was beckoning me impatiently to join him. That was easier said than done. The courtyard was a field of rocks, concrete rocks, that I had to clamber over to reach him.

When at last I was up there, the two of us stood, speechless, looking about in disbelief. The two great guns had been toppled over and lay on their sides, their barrels half buried in the marshes. All around us everything had been blasted to ruins. The remains of the buildings that must have housed the soldiers, and all the remnants of the concrete gun emplacement, littered the courtyard and the marshes beyond, as far as the eye could see.

But it was what had been left standing that amazed me, for the ancient stone walls of Lorenzo's beloved Camelot still stood, not entirely but mostly. The two of us touched fore-heads and held each other, neither of us wanting to let go of the other, nor of the moment.

Minutes later, I found myself sitting on our rock and telling him the story of how Arthur found the sword in the stone, and he was acting it out, drawing the sword out eas-ily, raising it high, then he was killing dragons again, and again.

"Agon agon!"

He knew and I knew that every dragon he was killing was a Nazi soldier, that all the wicked dragons were going or had gone. I could not help thinking, though, that one of them at least had been no dragon, but a friend we could trust, who had promised Maman and Papa would come home.

I clung to this promise, and to my belief now that Saint Sarah would help during the weeks that followed. With the Germans and the brown-shirted Milice gone, we could all go once again into town on market days. So we were there on the stall, selling our fish and our cheese, our honey and herbs, the tricolor flying high and proud again on the *mairie*, when the Americans arrived in a flurry of roaring jeeps and trucks. They really did smoke big fat cigars. What a day that was! The townspeople cheered and waved, and everyone kissed and hugged everyone else. We were free again to be us.

The Americans were so big and tall—that's what I remember most about them—and they laughed a lot. We had not seen or heard laughter like that in a very long time. And laughter, like joy, is infectious. They had chocolate too, which they handed out—Hershey Bars they called it—so I loved them for that too. Chocolate, cigarettes, and money to spend on the market stalls, on our stall as well—the Americans seemed to have everything. We could not understand what they were saying, of course, but that did not matter. Their smiles and ours said all that needed to be said. There was no more threat, no more fear. France was France again; France was ours again; France was free again!

But, despite all the euphoria in town that day, I could not forget that there was no Maman and Papa in the crowd. I never stopped looking for their faces, listening for their voices. When we came home to the farm, they were not there waiting for us. Henri and Nancy were still reassuring me that all would be well. Every day that Maman and Papa did not return, they told me the same thing again and again, but every day I believed them less. My hopes were fading. My faith was fragile.

There was some good news, though. Henri had made inquiries in town at the *mairie*, about the camp at Saliers where Maman and Papa had been taken, and they told him that Americans had liberated it, and were taking care of the prisoners. So I was hopeful again, for a few days. But in the end I did not believe that either. If it was so, where were Maman and Papa now? Why had they not come home? And then the nightmare thoughts would come again, that they had been taken away to other camps I had heard about. There was talk in the town of these other camps, far away, in Poland, in Germany, concentration camps they called them, where many people had been taken, where dreadful things had happened, where prisoners had been sent and did not return. Someone said Madame Salomon and her whole family had been taken to one of those, and no one had heard of them since.

My new Sully family enveloped me in love during these days of despair. I was never left alone with my dark thoughts. At night, we all still slept together in our one wide bed. Just being close to them gave me great comfort.

One night, I was lying there, only half awake, the others sleeping soundly beside me, when I heard a car drawing up outside. My first thought, irrational I know, was that the Germans were back. There were voices, and a loud knocking on the door downstairs. Henri was quickly awake and sitting up. He lit the lamp and went downstairs. We tried to follow him, but he told us all to wait on the stairs. He opened the door. From where we were at the top of the stairs, we could just about see.

Two soldiers in American uniforms were standing there. They had red crosses on their arms.

"Monsieur Henri Sully?" one of them said.

The soldiers were trying to speak French. We couldn't understand every word, but just enough. "You know these two, *monsieur*? They say they are Monsieur and Madame Charbonneau. They say they live here. Is that so?"

I was bounding down those stairs, and in their arms

before any more could be said. The two American soldiers had their answer. It was over there, right by the front door that it happened, Vincent, this homecoming, this longed-for moment, the very best moment of my entire life. ""

CHAPTER 30

Old Years Pass, New Years Come

"But, even as I clung to Maman and Papa, I knew they were not the same. I could feel Maman's shoulder blades through her coat, and, when I looked up into Papa's face, I saw his whole demeanour had changed. His eyes, once so bright, were sunken and sad, and I could see the white of his bones through his cheeks. They were pale, pale ghosts of their former selves. But they were alive and they were home, as the Caporal had promised us they would be. At that moment, nothing else in the world mattered to me.

Maman stayed poorly and weak for many months, but Papa grew better with every day that passed. His color returned, and his cheekbones disappeared as his dear face became more his own again. His energy came back, and the brightness in his eyes. Nancy brought them both back to life, feeding and caring for them, making sure they never lacked for food, or warmth, or comfort. Lorenzo would often sit with them, holding hands, touching foreheads, passing on his healing love to them. Henri and Nancy gave up their bedroom for them, so they could be together and quiet and with me, and they slept down here, in this room.

Maman and Papa said not a word to any of us—so far as I know, and certainly not to me—about the camp at Saliers. I learned only much later of the hunger and the suffering they and all the prisoners there had had to endure. Many had died of hunger and disease. I learned much later too that Madame Salomon and her family had died in Auschwitz, one family of six million Jews who had perished in the camps. Roma people had died in those camps too. Maman and Papa had been lucky. I had been lucky.

They did tell us of the day the Caporal had come to see them with a basket of food, with news of us all, and of the carousel. He told them that the war would be over soon, that they would be home again. He gave them new heart, new hope, they said, at a time they needed it most. Papa told me once when I was older that without the Caporal they might have faded away in that camp and died, as so many did, that they came home, at least in part, because of him.

In time, they both recovered, not fully in Maman's case. She was never as strong afterward, but the heart of her was there in her smile and laughter.

The Caporal not only helped bring me back my *maman* and *papa*, he gave us back our carousel too. The completion of the restoration of the carousel took a year or more after the war had ended. We all worked every day to make it just as fine and beautiful as it had once been. Nothing made Papa happier than to be carving the new rides, and nothing made Maman happier than to be painting them. It was the carousel as much as anything that gave them joy in life again.

Maman told me quite often afterward: "It was you, Kezia, the thought of you and the carousel, that your *papa* and I lived for in that dreadful camp. Then, when we came home, we watched you grow, and we saw the carousel coming together—that's what gave me back my life."

Then came the great day, the first of May in 1947. The carousel was finished. We loaded it up carefully, piece by piece, into a dozen or more farm carts, some belonging to neighbors, some to our relatives. Cheval pulled one of them, Honey another, whether she liked it or not. So, early in the morning, we set off down the farm track, past Camelot, and along the canal into town. Through the gateway under the walls of the town we went, past the church and into the town square.

We had the carousel up and working faster than we had ever done it before, and that was because there were so many helping hands. The queue to ride the Charbonneau Carousel that day stretched right around the square. They rang the church bells, and Monsieur Dubarry, the mayor—wearing his tricolor sash—made a long speech, which no one could hear, and to which no one was listening anyway, and then at last he gave the signal for Maman to start the music. With Lorenzo riding on his Val, and me at his side, and with every other ride full, the carousel began to turn, to the sound of "Sur le Pont d'Avignon," and to huge cheers and laughter from everyone there. There never was a day like it.

Alors, c'est presque la fin, almost the end of my story, Vincent. A couple of years later, Maman and Papa had built a new caravan, just like the old one, and painted it just the same too. So we had our own home again. I thought it would stay like that forever, the two families, the Sully family and the Charbonneau family, living side by side as we had before. But there is something in the heart of every Roma, Vincent: we have to keep moving on. I had changed, though. I think I had become used to being settled in one place, and Maman and Papa knew that. They could see I was happy where I was.

That was why—in part at least—they came to an arrangement with Nancy and Henri. I would stay at the farm. Nancy would go on schooling me, and Lorenzo and I, we would go on together as we had, like brother and sister, best of companions, dearest of friends. Maman and Papa would return to the farm every year in the spring and summer months to set up and run the carousel in town, and, while the season lasted, would live on the farm in the caravan as they had before.

They talked it all through with me and with Lorenzo one evening, all of us together in this room. I could not have been happier about it. I would have the best of both worlds: two families, both of whom I loved. And Lorenzo was—how do you say it?—over the moon. His celebratory flamingo dance that evening was the best, the most joyous he had ever danced.

Over the years, I became quite used to Maman and Papa coming and going through the spring and summer of every year. I would cycle into town and help them with the carousel as I had helped before. Sometimes I would travel with them in the caravan down to the sea at Saintes-Maries-de-la-Mer for the Roma festivals, and meet up with all my cousins, and aunts and uncles, who, mostly, very soon accepted Lorenzo, my Flamingo Boy brother, as one of the family. And, if some of them didn't, I didn't care anyway. I just wouldn't speak to them again.

The seasons passed. The summers came and went, the mosquitoes and the mistral winds, the flamingos nesting out on the islands in the spring, the fledglings flying. And Lorenzo and I—well, we grew up, as Maman and Papa, and Nancy and Henri, grew older. Maman, her heart weakened by her time in the camp, died first, then Henri a few years later. It happens this way, Vincent, it always has. The old fade away, and we take their place.

Old years pass, new years come, and now Lorenzo and I find ourselves alone here, working the farm as best we can. Two of my younger cousins look after the carousel these days—so it's still the Charbonneau Carousel—and they bring it to Aigues-Mortes in the spring and summer months, just as we always did. And Lorenzo and I still go in on market days sometimes and run our stall, when we have enough to sell. So Lorenzo still gets his ride on his Val from time to time, and I get to see the children riding around, and hear their laughter. And every ride still begins with "Sur le Pont d'Avignon" on the barrel organ.

Every time I'm there, I see Elephant and Bull and Dragon and Horse, and all the others, and I remember it was Papa who carved every one of them. When I look closely, I can see Papa's chisel marks and Maman's brushstrokes on them, as if they made them yesterday. Maman and Papa, they live on in the carousel, and in me. So, that's our story done, Vincent. Now you know everything. Bedtime, I think. "

CHAPTER 31

Last Words

"Except that I don't know everything," I told her. "You still haven't answered my question. You never told me how come you speak such good English, did you?"

"*Zut alors!*" Kezia laughed. "I forgot. I am getting old. I forgot, and you remembered. *Eh bien*, well, as I told you already, I think, there was another Englishman who turned up at our door, over thirty years ago now, not young like you. He was a professor, an ornithologist. Dr. Alan Roberts he was called. At the time, we had a severe problem on the marshes here—not just here, but all over the Camargue. The flamingos were becoming fewer and fewer. Many years they did not come to breed here on our lakes at all. There was a real danger that soon there would be no flamingos breeding and living in the Camargue anymore. The Camargue without flamingos was unthinkable to us.

"We all knew this, but did not know what to do about it. There were many reasons. In dry springs and dry summers, when the water in the lakes was low, the foxes and wild boar and badgers could get across to the breeding islands, and kill the sitting flamingos and their chicks in the nests. So, more and more, the flamingos were not coming to breed here, and were breeding elsewhere, where it was safer. They are not stupid. Over the years, of course, the stealing of flamingo eggs had done and was still doing a lot of damage too.

So anyway, this Englishman—this Professor Alan Roberts—arrived at our door one day. He told us he was passionate about the survival of flamingos in the Camargue, and he needed somewhere to stay out on the marshes, so he could make his research, do his work. He had heard about this "Flamingo Boy," who, he had been told, lived here in this house, who knew more about flamingos than anyone else around. He wanted to meet him, to work with him, so that they could share their knowledge, and together help save the flamingos of the Camargue.

So the two met, Alan and Lorenzo. And Alan stayed— for five years or more. He slept where you now sleep, and every day he and Lorenzo would be out on the marshes, observing the flamingos, photographing them, studying them, working out what could be done— had to be done— to save them. All those photos of the flamingos you see on the walls, it was Alan who took them. A wonderful photographer! And, while he stayed, Nancy asked him to teach me English. Nancy was always the teacher. Her mantra was "the more you know, Kezia, the better you grow." She was right too. They did a deal: he would give me lessons instead of paying rent for his room. So that's what happened. *Alors*, now you know: that was how I learned English, Vincent.

Meanwhile, Alan, along with Lorenzo, and with many others here all over the region who love our flamingos, devised a plan. Laws should be made to prevent the theft of flamingo eggs. It was done. Water levels were to be regulated, so there was always enough water in the marshes to keep the flamingos safe from predators on their breeding islands. Predators were to be controlled. This was all done too. But, by now, most of the flamingos had already deserted their breeding islands, and, in spite of all these efforts, very few flamingos were returning to the Camargue to breed. It looked as if it was all too late.

Then Lorenzo had an idea, a brilliant idea. He went out in the boat one day with Alan onto the island in our lake, and showed Alan what must be done, on this island, and on all the islands, if we wanted the flamingos to return. Out of the mud Lorenzo crafted with his own hands an imitation of a flamingo nest, a raised mound of mud, with a dip in the top for the eggs to rest in. This, Lorenzo was sure—and Alan was soon persuaded too—was the best chance of encouraging the flamingos to come back in numbers and lay their eggs. Provide them with ready-made, purpose-built nests made of mud, make it look as if they had been there from the year before, and from the year before that, that this was their place. They had to feel they were coming home.

*

"The two of them, Lorenzo and Alan," continued Kezia, "spent days, weeks, months out there, crafting hundreds of these nests of mud. I made some too myself. And the next year, in April, many more flamingos flew in, and the year after that they returned in the hundreds, then in the thousands all over the Camargue. It is really true, *c'est vraiment vrai*, I'm telling you. And, as you hear, I speak English too, quite well, *n'est-ce pas*? Are you happy now, Vincent? And I was thinking—are you fit for an outing tomorrow?"

"Yes," I said. "Where are we going?"

"To market. It is market day tomorrow in town, and I think you are well enough now to come with us. We shall see the carousel turning, hear Maman's barrel organ. How would you like that?"

I hardly slept a wink that night—an eighteen-year-old boy so excited over the prospect of seeing a carousel. Hardly cool, is it?

They had a car. It was ridiculous, I know, but I really had imagined we would be going by horse and cart. Instead, we drove to town in a bouncy French car made of corrugated tin, with an engine that sounded like my mother's old sewing machine at home. We drove down the farm track along the canal, over the bridge, and there ahead of me was the walled town of Aigues-Mortes. We parked outside the town walls and walked in under the great gateway into the crowded streets. I could already hear a barrel organ playing. Sure enough it was "Sur le Pont d'Avignon." Lorenzo was humming along happily to the music, clapping his hands.

There at last I had my first sight of it, in the town square, the carousel turning, turning. The square was full of people browsing the market stalls, watching the carousel, strolling the streets, sitting in the cafés. Kezia introduced me to her cousins and friends as "the English friend Lorenzo had found half dead in the marshes." I liked that.

It was awhile before the carousel stopped, and Lorenzo and I could get on. I rode Elephant because Lorenzo said I should, and he rode Val, of course. Everyone else on the ride was a child, but no one seemed to mind us being there. Everyone knew Lorenzo, and I was with Flamingo Boy—as he was still known—so it was fine. Then "Sur le Pont d'Avignon" was playing on the barrel organ again, and the carousel was turning, turning. I don't think I had ever been on a carousel before. I loved every minute of it, Lorenzo's uninhibited joy, and the music, especially the music. It was truly a resplendent, magical, glorious thing, this carousel.

As it turned and turned, I was remembering everything, the whole history of the carousel, of the family who had made it, of everything that had happened in this square. The story behind it all came back to me, and I lived it again in my mind. When it stopped, I wanted to have another go at once. But there were dozens of other children waiting to get on—young children, proper children, not like me.

I was sitting there on Elephant, rather reluctant to get off, when something happened that I shall never forget as long as I live. Lorenzo was mounted on Horse and I noticed he was unusually still, perfectly still, as if in some kind of trance. I thought at first this might be a sign that he was going to have a fit—I had seen them begin like this before, like the calm before a storm. But then he got off Horse, climbed down from the carousel, and started walking determinedly into the crowd of people, who parted for him as he came through. I followed him with Kezia. He was walking toward the *mairie*.

Outside the *mairie* I saw an old man standing there on his own. He was leaning heavily on a stick, watching Lorenzo coming toward him. Everyone in the square knew something very strange was happening. Silence had fallen. Lorenzo walked right up to the old man and looked him in the face. He reached out and touched his hair, his face, then smelled his fingers.

"Capo?" he said. "Capo?"

The old man nodded. There were tears running down his face. "Willi Brenner, Lorenzo," he replied. "Or Capo Capo, whichever you like."

Then Kezia was there, the three of them together, arms around one another.

I stood and watched. Before my eyes, the story had come full circle.

Kezia turned and called me over. I shook his hand. He was still tall, if a little bent. His hair was white, what there was of it. Lorenzo could not stop touching his face, his hair.

So I was there when Willi Brenner reached into his pocket and gave it back to Kezia, the scorched fragment of the icon of Saint Sarah. "I brought this back," he said. "You must keep it now. It has looked after me, as I think you wanted it to. It is yours. It always was. **"**

And this is the true end of the story, the end of the road. With Kezia's encouragement, and at Lorenzo's insistence, I stayed in the Camargue, helped out on the farm, never went to college or university. I settled here and, many years later, I wrote this book. While I was writing, Kezia told me I should always keep their precious fragment of the icon of Saint Sarah beside me all the time—to guide my hand, she said.

So I had it with me when I began writing this some months ago, sitting on the beach in Saintes-Maries-de-la-Mer, the beach where, I discovered, Vincent van Gogh had sat and painted his picture of the four boats, the same beach where Kezia told me they had found all those planks of wood. And I came back here today to sit on the beach, and finish it, to write these last words of my story, the icon on the sand beside me. This seemed the right place to do it. Full circle again. I like full circles.

I think it was no accident that Vincent van Gogh had called one of those fishing boats he painted *Amitié*— friendship.

He had sought friendship all his life, and died from the lack of it. I have been luckier, much luckier. I followed the bend in the road that began in Watford all those long years ago, and it led me here. I have found friendship, a home too, and much more besides, here, in this wild and wonderful place of flying pink flamingos.